Young Captain Barney

Young

Captain

Barney

by RICHARD W. EDMONDS

H
10

Ed 577 y

MACRAE SMITH COMPANY PHILADELPHIA 1956

I am indebted to Lieutenant M. V. Brewington, U.S.N.R., for his generous help with design and rigging of ships of colonial days.

Library of Congress Catalog Card Number 56-6182

564

Manufactured in the United States of America

FOREWORD

MOST OF THE CONVERSATIONS AND MANY OF THE CHARACTERS in this story are fictitious, but Joshua Barney is historical and this is a fairly true and faithful account of his exploits during the first five years of his life afloat. No writer of fiction would dare to create such a character, for without the well-authenticated record he would be completely unbelievable, but Barney was intensely real. As a seaman he was certainly a genius and he had a rare gift for leadership and a personality that captivated men and women of all ages and all walks of life. It is a strange quirk of history that he has been so nearly forgotten, for he was famous not only in the colonies but over much of Europe before he was twenty-five years of age. But fame has ever been a fickle jade, and Barney fell short of the sort of greatness that would endear him to historians. His most painstaking biographer called him a Sailor of Fortune, and no better description of him could be put into three words. He lived always at a reckless pace and died young, but in my opinion he deserves better than he has received from history.

R.W.E.

TO MY WIFE

Young Captain Barney

CHAPTER ONE

THE UPPER HALL WAS COLD IN SPITE OF THE GREAT LOG FIRES
that still blazed in the wide fireplaces of the first floor, and
Joshua shivered in his flannel nightshirt as he crouched at
the head of the stairs and watched his father in the hall
below.

Yawning mightily, William Barney closed the massive
front door on the last of his departing guests.

'Tis my last chance, the boy thought. I've got to go now.
Still he tarried, dreading the outcome. To his right, the
stair well cut across the hem of his mother's skirt as she
came into the parlor doorway. " 'Tis almost dawn, William," she said. She patted a yawn. "And I'm half dead for
sleep."

"Aye, we're getting old, my dear." William yawned
again.

I've got to go now, Joshua told himself again. He felt a
little sick at heart to think how completely his whole future depended upon his father's present uncertain temper. He rose and started down the stairs, his bare feet
padding silently, his long nightshirt trailing on the treads
behind him, his brilliant dark eyes intent on his father's
tired face.

"Yes, William," he heard his mother's reply, "we are.

And all these holiday parties———" She broke off as she followed her husband's eyes and saw the boy descending the stairs.

"What is the meaning of this, young man?" his father asked. "Why aren't you asleep in your bed?"

"I have got to talk to you, sir. 'Tis about Mr. Welch."

"Tomorrow, Joshua. Tomorrow."

"Tomorrow I was to return to the countinghouse, sir. And you haven't had a minute for me since I've been home, sir. Not a minute."

Mother and father exchanged a significant glance, for they had feared something of this sort from the moment Joshua had arrived for the Christmas holidays, and they had been surprised and relieved as the days had passed without it.

"Come in to the fire, then," William said in a tone of resignation. When a man has fourteen children he must endure much. He led the way into the disorderly parlor. Rugs were rolled up and chairs pushed back against the walls, and empty glasses littered the tables and mantel. His father took one chair and Joshua another and they drew them to the fire, the boy's ridiculous nightshirt with its faded pink flowers flapping as he moved. William and Frances seated themselves, and William yawned again.

"Well?" he said, blinking tears of sleepiness out of his eyes and regarding Joshua with a frown of vexation.

The boy, his bare feet planted a little apart, stood beside his father's chair. His glance went first to his mother's troubled brown eyes, then back to meet his father's frowning gaze. For months he had been planning for this moment, but he had never visualized himself playing his part dressed like this. He had laboriously prepared and carefully rehearsed a speech that to him seemed a masterpiece of eloquence.

"I have been in Mr. Welch's countinghouse for a year, sir," he began. "I hate it. 'Tis no fit work for a man."

William interrupted him with a snort. "For a *man*, did you say, boy?"

Joshua paused, but now that action was joined he was no longer nervous. He had been so deeply in earnest that it had never occurred to him that his father would find anything ridiculous in his speech, but he saw with startling clarity that all the rest of it would be brushed aside with the same scorn. While he swiftly revised his tactics he stood with his feet squarely on the floor, his toes bearing down hard as if to dig in against any effort to dislodge him. Clearly this was no time for skirmishing, so after the briefest pause he staked everything on a frontal attack. "I will not go back to it unless you command me, sir," he said.

It was the luckiest, or the shrewdest, answer he could have made, for William was a kind and indulgent father who never willingly used compulsion on any of his children. Thoughtfully, for a moment, he studied the boy's earnest face, and he found himself surprised all over again at the compelling power of those brilliant dark eyes. Either he had forgotten how intense they could be, or a year in Alexandria had given them added force. He crossed his right leg over his left, and moved his head in a peculiar little sidewise mannerism he had. "You are still determined to go to sea, my son?" he asked reluctantly.

"Yes, sir!"

"Oh, but Joshua!" There were pain and anxiety in his mother's voice. "You're still so young!"

"I'm going on twelve, ma'am!" Joshua replied with all the dignity his flowered nightshirt would permit. "And besides, Papa promised, you know, ma'am."

"When you could . . ." She stopped suddenly.

"Yes, ma'am! When I could take care of myself. And I've been doing it for fifteen months, now!"

"There is more to taking care . . ." William suddenly realized that he was about to offer the boy a challenge that would only harden his resolution, and as quickly as his weary wits permitted, he changed his tactics. "Mr. Welch says you are doing fine work, son," he said with an attempt at heartiness that he thought must sound hollow even to a boy's ears. "He tells me you have a rare fine head for the mathematics and he hopes to advance you. Mayhap you will like the work when you get deeper into it. I had hoped you were settling into the job and forgetting the sea."

"No, sir! Never! I hate the countinghouse! Grubbing away like a worm in a dark hole! 'Tis the sea I want, sir! Try me at it. I'll not disappoint you, sir."

William sighed. "Very well, son," he said reluctantly. "I will see what arrangements I can make for you."

"Thank you, sir," Joshua replied, striving to maintain an air of dignified calm before his parents; but his dancing eyes and the relief and delight that showed plainly in his expressive face belied his efforts. "I'll not disappoint you, sir," he repeated. There was more warmth than usual in the good-night kisses he bestowed on his parents; but he turned, then, and walked sedately to the door. At that point, however, his self-restraint was abandoned. He shot through the doorway, his nightshirt held high in front, and he tore up the stairs like a whirlwind, shouting to his sleeping brothers and sisters as he went.

"Will! Mary! Johnnie! Peg! I'm to be a sea captain!" His voice was shrill with excitement. "Father has consented! I'm going to sea! I'm to be master of a tall ship!"

William smiled at his wife. "He acts mighty old when he has something on his mind," he said, a rueful note in his voice, "but he's still just a little boy for all that."

Tears sparkled in Frances' eyes. "Yes, William, just a little boy. Much too young to go to sea. His boldness and self-confidence will surely get him into trouble. Couldn't you have kept him in the countinghouse at least for another year?"

"I don't believe so, Fran. I saw Mr. Welch in Baltimore today. This is the first chance I've had to tell you about it. I didn't tell Joshua all he said. 'Twould only have strengthened his hand. Mr. Welch did say the boy had a rare fine head for the mathematics and is a hard worker, but he also said he manages to keep the other boys in such an uproar with his deviltry that he really doesn't know how he could stand much more of him. You can't bottle up a boy like that. He's explosive. 'Tis better to put him under good masters than to have him run away."

The next day William called for his horse and rode into Baltimore, where he saw his old friend, Obediah Chilton, captain of the Chesapeake Bay pilot boat, *Gallant Mary*, and after much discussion they reached a decision.

"You say the lad is but eleven years of age, William?"

"Aye, but large and strong for his years." He almost said "headstrong," but caught himself just in time.

"Well, William, I'll try him. But 'tis young. Another

year or two on him would do him no harm, but I'll try
him. You are right not to prentice him. Just let him try
it out. As you say, if he starts in January and sticks it
through February and March—aye, we'll soon see."

So it was settled. Joshua suffered none of the qualms
that assailed his mother, his father and, to a lesser degree,
Captain Chilton. And on an icy dawn a few days later
he rode into Baltimore in a farm wagon. With his oak
sea chest heavy on his shoulder he stepped sure-footed
over the deep, frozen ruts of Water Street to Mr. Smith's
West Pier. He was oblivious of the cold wind that blew
down Gay Street, and of the rough timbers, scarred by
iron-shod hoofs and wagon wheels, on which he walked.
For there above the end of the pier stood the two rakish
masts of the vessel on which he was about to sail.

The morning sun was scarcely above the horizon on his
left when he set his sea chest on the hand-hewn stringer
at the end of the pier and stood for a few minutes running
his eyes over the rigging and the sturdy hull of the little
vessel. He set the spread finger tips of his left hand rigidly
on the timber and dropped lightly to the gently-heaving
deck. He lifted his chest and set it down, crossed the deck,
slid back the hatch cover and climbed down the ladder
into the cabin.

As he went down, he sank into a powerful odor that
surrounded and engulfed him. He recognized the rancid
reek of bodies and clothing long unwashed, and the biting
fumes of country-twist tobacco—for the combination was
nothing new to him. In the past year he had missed no
opportunity to board ships in the busy port of Alexandria
and talk to the sailors, and he had found the same reek

in all forecastles. It was part of the life at sea, and he accepted it without question.

His feet found the deck at the foot of the ladder, and he peered eagerly into the shadows about him. For a vessel that had looked so small from the pier, she now seemed cavernous, for there was not a bulkhead in her, and his eyes would require a few minutes to adjust themselves to the gloom. Dim and shadowy she was, and filled with a mystery that was as exciting as her odor was powerful— on this vessel he was to sail away to the wide open reaches of the Chesapeake and the vast, invisible future.

"Shut that hatch!" said a man who sat hunched over a table to Joshua's left, the tip of a tall quill pen waggling steadily just beyond his right shoulder.

"Aye, aye, sir," Joshua responded readily, and he reached overhead and slid-to the hatch cover with a bang. Now the vessel was even darker, for the only light came from the Betty lamp just beyond the man's head.

The man laid down his quill and swung around.

"Joshua Barney reporting for duty, sir," the boy said.

"H-m-m-m. So you are Joshua Barney, eh?" One keen gray eye sparkled in the light the Betty lamp threw on the right side of the captain's face. The left side of his face remained in shadow. From fore and aft, as Joshua approached, the shadows pressed close upon the man and the boy, and there between light and shadow was the bold, imperious, hawklike profile of the captain in plain view, at the same time that his full face looked squarely at the boy. It was a compelling face, such a face as a boy could delight to serve under. To Joshua's eager imagination the moment had a strangely eerie and delightful quality com-

17

pounded of light and shadows, a commanding presence and an odor that meant the sea and the knowledge that he was about to sail. It was a moment rich with promise of an exciting career.

"Yes, sir," Joshua said calmly enough. The gray eyes of the captain—the sparkling one and the shadowed one— were giving him a most penetrating scrutiny, and he felt it but was not disturbed. It was, after all, a friendly scrutiny, and there was nothing bashful about the boy.

"Your father said you were only eleven."

"Going on for twelve, sir. I was born the sixth of July, 1759."

"You look older."

"Yes, sir."

"So you want to follow the sea!"

"Yes, sir!"

" 'Tis a hard life, boy. Do you know what you'll have to do on this vessel?"

"Handle lines, sir. Reef sails. Furl 'em. Stand my trick at the tiller."

The captain's eyebrows rose slightly. "Are you planning to start right in as a seaman, without so much as a term as cabin boy, to get your sea legs and toughen yourself?"

"I hope so, sir!" He had given much earnest thought to this point. He knew that so small a vessel had no need for a cabin boy, and he was fiercely resolved to avoid that lowly rating if he could.

"Do you think you can keep your feet on an icy deck that's tilting in all directions at once? Handle lines like iron bars for ice? And sails like sheet iron for the same reason? And do it all with green water pouring down the deck? And come right out of the inside of a counting-house in the worst time of the year, with no chance to harden yourself in mild weather? Do you, now? Eh?"

"I do, sir."

"Well, and do you think I'll be mad enough to let my friend's son try it, and die of a cold on the lungs? Tell me that, now."

"I'm pretty tough, sir. Really I am."

The captain shifted the lamp shade so that the light shone more fully on the boy's face and regarded him intently for a moment. He saw conviction in the brilliant dark eyes. He saw, too, that the boy was massively built, with a broad, deep chest, heavy shoulders and thick neck, and a ruddy glow in his skin that suggested immense vitality. His features were all large, especially his nose, which was high and long—a bold, aggressive nose. He was hardly a handsome lad. In fact, barring his remarkable eyes he was not handsome at all, but he looked mature and thoughtful for his years. The captain looked him all over and then his glance was drawn back to those compelling eyes, and he sensed in them an unusual power and a lively intelligence.

Joshua's bearing throughout this frank appraisal gave no hint of the anxiety he felt. He bore the scrutiny without swagger and without self-consciousness, considerably encouraged that so far, at least, the captain's words left him hope that he might escape the rating of cabin boy.

In forty years at sea, before he had retired to the comparative ease of the little pilot boat, Captain Chilton had commanded many men and not a few boys, and he rather fancied himself as a judge of character. Mayhap, he thought, this boy was just half as good as his father thought he was. If he was—just half—he'd not lose a good friend on account of him. To Joshua he said, "Pretty cocky for a youngster, aren't you, Barney?"

"Cocky?" The boy looked surprised and chagrined. "I hope not, sir!"

"We'll soon see," said the captain. "There's mighty little you'll hide from your shipmates." Facing into the shadows forward, he called, "Mr. Dodge! This is Joshua Barney. He'll be sailing with us."

"Aye, aye, sir," came the reply. "Step forrard, Barney."

The captain had left the all-important question wide open, and Barney felt with elation that from this moment he was on trial and it was for him, by his conduct and bearing, to determine whether or not he would start as cabin boy. With this thought in his mind he picked his way around a massive brick pillar built amidships.

"Give that fiah a poke as you come by, Barney," said the same voice from the shadows. "We'll have a bit of light."

Turning, Joshua saw that the tapering brick pillar was a fireplace, and that a few logs smoldered on the hearth. Spits and a crane and the remnants of several well-gnawed fowl carcasses indicated clearly not only that this was the galley, but that breakfast had been finished but a short time ago.

Joshua pushed the glowing noses of the logs together, heaped on fresh kindling and blew the coals to a bright flame. The firelight revealed that the forward part of the vessel was lined with double-decked bunks, eight of them, converging forward. Midway between the galley and the forepeak, the foremast came down through the deck, and served the extra duty of clothes hanger, being ringed around with heavily-laden hooks.

Faces peered at Joshua from the shadows of the bunks,

where the crew sprawled, awaiting the ebb tide. The men saw a lad who appeared to be all of thirteen years of age, and as it was common practice for the sailing vessels of the day to carry cabin boys of that age, they saw nothing odd in the situation. Cabin boys were useful in more ways than appeared in their papers, especially when, as on most ships, they were broken to unquestioning obedience right from the start. Joshua had talked to enough sailors in the busy port of Alexandria to know that, and he was on guard against it. Consequently, when a black-browed young fellow in an upper bunk scowled down at him and commanded peremptorily, "Heave me up them boots, boy," Joshua retorted, "Get 'em yourself. I'm no cabin boy."

Without a word the sailor dropped to the deck and swung his open palm at Joshua's head. The boy ducked with the skill and speed developed in many a rough-and-tumble with his older brothers and with the boys of his little backwoods school, and all in one smooth, fast motion he came up with the heavy galley poker cocked back at arm's length.

The man in the nearest bunk reached out swiftly and wrenched it from Joshua's hand, then heaved himself to his feet and stood between the boy and the astonished sailor.

"There'll be no boys beat up on this vessel, Pete," he said. "See you remember that. We don't do things that-a-way."

Joshua smiled at him. "I guess you saved me a right good beating, mister," he said, "but I think I'd have landed one good one, anyway."

The man gave Joshua a long, searching look which the boy returned, entirely unruffled—gray eyes and dark ones sparkling in the leaping firelight.

"I'm Mr. Dodge, lad," he said. "Pete's as new as you be, an' just has some deep-sea notions, seems like. But we got a good captain, an' fellers that don't get along here, we just set 'em ashore, which ain't never far away. You won't have no trouble on this vessel—that is, if you ain't cocky or quarrelsome, an' don't get too big for yore britches."

"That's fine. Any time you catch me starting a quarrel, just set me ashore. And I'll always take orders in line of duty."

"You'd a dog sight better had. You got a chest?"

"Yes, sir."

"Go get it. Put it under Ab Wade's la'b'd bunk, amidships, there. You take the upper."

Having thus halted the quarrel and disposed of all current business, the mate subsided on his bunk again.

Joshua's sea chest, built of solid oak, was heavy, but he tied a rope through the handle in one end and lowered it easily through the hatch. Nobody said a word to him. He shoved his chest under the lower bunk indicated by Mr. Dodge and then, since he had no choice but to stand up or lie down, he climbed to his bunk and stretched out. He was eager to go on deck, but after all, there was nothing to do there and besides he shrewdly guessed it would be better to do exactly as the rest of the crew did.

A gentle swell lifted the vessel and let her down, and set her to tugging a bit at her lines and rubbing her heavy mats against the pilings. To every slight motion and sound she made, Joshua listened and thrilled. Every gentle heave of the bunk under him, every creak of timber, every little slap and slosh of water just outside that single wall of planks—every minute detail that bespoke the sea—was an unalloyed delight.

Occasionally footsteps sounded on the deck, the hatch opened and slammed shut. Captain Chilton greeted each newcomer by his first name, but none of them came forward, and Joshua realized that these were the pilots returning from their holiday ashore, and that they would bunk aft with the captain. They greeted each other in the strong-timbred voices of seamen, but they spoke almost entirely of their families and their holidays, and Joshua was disappointed that there was no talk of the sea.

The sailors lay quiet in their bunks, apparently dozing until time to make sail. Joshua's impatience mounted until he could wait no longer. He climbed down and pulled on his heavy pea jacket.

"I'll just go on deck and see what she looks like," he said to the mate with his flashing smile. "I've waited a long time for this."

"Sea-struck, huh? You ain't had time to wait long for anything. Mind you don't fall overboard."

"Likely Pete'll haul me out if I do," Joshua retorted with a laugh, and climbed the ladder, slamming the hatch behind him.

Conversation broke out at once.

"You could easy beat the stuffin' out of that nipper," said the mate, "but you shore ain't a-goin' to scare him. I tell ye, I seen a red fire in them black eyes of his. Pete, if ye so much as lay a hand on that boy, time I get through with you, you'll wish I'd just keel-hauled you instead."

"Haw!" snorted Luke Prentis, "ye got that back'ards, Harry. Ye better tell that boy to lay offen Pete!"

A shout of delighted laughter greeted that sally, and Pete grinned sheepishly.

"Quickest thing ever I did see," Absalom Wade chuckled, "way he grabbed that poker. An' wa'n't even flustered. Jes's quiet an' easy when 'twas over as kiss m' lady's hand."

"I got nothin' agin the boy," said Pete. "He's jes' a mite too big for his britches. He needs to be fitted into 'em."

"Maybe so. Maybe not. That ain't the point. The point is, you're a hand here, same's he is. You leave him to me."

CHAPTER TWO

"TURN OUT, SAILOR. WE'RE GOIN' OUTSIDE." A HEARTY THUMP-
ing on the under side of his sailcloth bunk drove the words
into Joshua's sleeping mind.

"Sailor!" Eagerly he seized the word while his wits bat-
tled sleep. No cabin boy. A sailor! A sailor, going outside!
Outside the bay! He sat up so suddenly he cracked his
forehead a shattering blow against a deck beam. He collapsed, stunned for a moment, and pains rioted through
his head. But a sailor was above pain. Nothing stopped
him. Joshua set his teeth hard and rolled over. His eyes
met the mate's inquiring glance, but neither spoke and the
boy peered down to make sure he didn't step on Absalom's
neck, then lowered himself to the deck. He need not have
been so careful. Ab, already dressed, was hard at work
cooking breakfast. Harry, Job and Luke were dressing
rapidly and talking cheerfully about the aroma of food
their discriminating noses could detect in spite of the early
morning reek of the forecastle. The pain in his head was
bad but Joshua said nothing as he dressed, and it began to
subside.

Two long spits were set on hooks across the galley fire
and on each spit a few wild fowl, ducks and geese, were

broiling as Ab turned them. In the ashes of the hearth fish were cooking. Meals aboard a Chesapeake Bay pilot boat were always lavish, for nature supplied everything in boundless abundance. The crew had only to reach out and take what it wanted. Wild geese, ducks, oysters, trout, rock, crabs and Norfolk spot were not delicacies—they were staple articles of diet.

Joshua, the pain almost gone from his forehead, ate doggedly, determined to conceal the heaving sensation the odor was causing in his stomach. It was a part of the life. He'd just have to get used to it.

A long, narrow, purple swelling was growing on his forehead, but nobody mentioned it.

When he felt that he had forced down a reasonable amount of food, he put on his heavy pea jacket and set his hat on his head, but when it touched his bruised forehead, it felt so hard he quickly removed it. He tried tilting it forward but that brought it down on his nose, so he tilted it far back and knew at once that the first breeze would carry it away. At that moment he caught the mate's gray eyes on him and he grinned. "Guess I don't need a hat today," he said, tossed it onto his bunk, and went hurriedly on deck.

In the pure air his stomach settled down and he looked about him with mounting delight. A few clouds were banked along the eastern horizon, but the sky overhead was clear, and the sun was rising in a blaze of glory. A fresh breeze swayed the tops of the dense stand of pines to the north, eddied down, and flawed the waters of the little cove. Between the vessel and the wooded shore, from the point of Willoughby Spit all the way around the cove, the water swarmed with ducks busy with their feeding

and very garrulous about it. Joshua paid no more attention to them than he paid to the hens in his father's yard
at home; they were much too common a sight. He was
interested in the weather, and he saw that the day would
be fine.

Captain Chilton came on deck, and after him, the crew.
Blocks squealed as halliards ran through them, and
sails slatted loosely.

"Up anchor," the captain ordered.

The *Gallant Mary* had no capstan, and the crew strained
on the dripping anchor cable.

"Hove short!" Harry sang out from the bow.

"Heave 'er up and sheet home!"

Under the light pressure of the wind that eddied down
over the tall pines the *Gallant Mary* lost her slight headway and began drifting astern. Captain Chilton put the
tiller hard over; the vessel circled as she backed and swung
her bow to the west. Joshua watched every motion avidly.
The sails filled and the sheets banged taut. The vessel
heeled a little under the wind's light pressure. She started
slowly ahead, then more swiftly, and in a moment she
was slipping sweetly through the sheltered waters of
Willoughby Bay. The tiny waves slapped her bows and
upturned starboard side with merry little chuckling sounds
that the boy found utterly delightful. Beyond the sheltering pines she caught the full force of the wind and heeled
far over. She leaped ahead. She slashed through the turbulence of the James River and sent clouds of spray flying aft.

"Keep yo' hands in yo' pockets 'til they dry off, boy,"
Harry Dodge told Joshua. "Day like today, they'll freeze
quick when they're wet."

Joshua wiped his hands on the front of his pea jacket, surprised to find how numb they were. He had been too absorbed to notice. He jammed them into his pockets, and pains soon stabbed them as the warm blood flowed again.

"Luke, take the tiller," Captain Chilton ordered.

Someday, Joshua thought, he'll let me do that. Steering, he thought, must be the noblest job a man could have. He wondered that captains could be so generous with the privilege. For the hours that a man was the helmsman he had complete control of the vessel. All her tons of cunningly-fashioned timber, her taut cordage humming in the wind, her sails and spars—all her intricate and beautiful mechanism—were brainless and dead if her helmsman so much as lifted his hand from the tiller. The brain of the helmsman was the brain of the ship; the rest of the crew were no more than her fingers and toes.

The pilot boat ran out of the James into the Chesapeake and tacked away to the north. On this tack she slogged into the seas, close-hauled. The crew wore their tarred canvas clothes, and Joshua had his on, too. They were so stiff he had difficulty moving about, and so bulky that he had to walk with the spread-legged gait of a veteran seaman. There was no doubt he needed them, though, for heavy showers of spray blew down the deck, along with smoke and sparks from the chimney amidships, and now and then the bow took a big bite out of a wave and green water, white-laced, poured down the deck and out through the lee scuppers.

Joshua found that by looking forward he could see no land at all—only tossing, whitecapped seas. So it would be on all sides of him when, from the deck of a great ship, he would have watched the shore line sink below the horizon astern. For days and weeks on end there would be only the restless, ever-moving sea. Astern now, if he turned his head, there was a strip of white beach topped by dark green pines; but it wasn't too difficult to forget that beach and think only of wide, wide seas and distant ports.

Captain Chilton put the vessel on another tack, due east. An hour later the *Gallant Mary* passed between the Virginia capes and sailed out upon the Atlantic Ocean.

How vast was the sea! The horizon was a dim line incredibly far away. It curved around with the little vessel as its center. If he sailed far enough due east, would he come up with it? And would there be another horizon on beyond? No, probably not. No, almost certainly not. The horizon would surely move along ahead of him. It would come along astern. It was just as far as he could see, and it would stay that distance away from him always. And this vast circle of sea and sky—why, it was just a small fraction of the whole vast sea and sky! His father said the earth was round, but it didn't look round. It looked flat. On the plantation there was always something to shut off the view, but here there was nothing, and his imagination struggled with the problems set up by the immensity of the sea and the sky.

"Job for a pilot," Luke called, his eyes on the eastern horizon.

Joshua searched the sea. The sun was high now, and the horizon was a line unbroken by the early morning glare, but he saw nothing. He didn't like to say so, though, so he continued to search that part of the sea on which more experienced eyes were fixed until he perceived a tiny smudge which he decided might be a sail.

An hour passed. Topsails and courses rose above the horizon, gained size and definition.

The *Gallant Mary* was hove-to, awaiting the incoming vessel. All of the latter's sails were above the horizon, and her black hull crept into view. Joshua watched fascinated as the stranger that had come clear across the Atlantic bore down upon him.

A few men moved, monkeylike, far aloft; a few heads and shoulders appeared above the rail. To windward of the *Gallant Mary,* and within speaking distance, the brig backed her topsails and came to a full stop. Joshua was fascinated by the maneuver. He immediately perceived that half the brig's sail power had been set to drive aft, while the other half continued to drive forward, and the result was a stalemate. His interest was written plainly on his face.

"You see what he's done there, Barney?" Captain Chilton asked, wondering if the boy really did understand as clearly as he appeared to.

"Why, yes, sir," Joshua replied eagerly. "He didn't shift any but his big topsails and he's still right ker-slap-dab on his course. He couldn't have done it simpler, could he, sir?"

"Couldn't possibly."

Joshua's eyes lingered a moment on the boat that came dancing across the seas to pick up a pilot, then shifted back to the brig. Over his head the captain's eyes met the mate's in a long glance and his eyebrows lifted slightly. Dodge nodded with a look of deep satisfaction.

A few days later Captain Chilton called Joshua aft.

"Your father said you were good at keeping books, Barney," he said.

"I did it for a whole year, sir. I am well out of it. 'Tis no fit work for a man."

A suggestion of a smile quirked the corners of the captain's lips.

"Did you know books have to be kept aboard ship?"

"The logbook? Yes, sir."

"You might call it a log, though we don't keep a regular log like a seagoing vessel. We keep a record of pilots supplied and taken off. Pilot fees collected. Expenses. I was wondering if you'd think that worthy of a man."

"Oh, yes, sir! That's different!"

So Joshua was initiated into the simple mysteries of a pilot boat's account book. He spent, perhaps, half an hour at the captain's table that day.

Daily thereafter he went aft and worked on the captain's accounts. Finding only a few minutes of work to do on them, he started jotting down brief observations on weather such as he fancied would be appropriate to a seagoing log. When Captain Chilton made no objection, he enlarged the notations to include time at which sails were sighted, the course on which the pilot boat had been sailing at the moment, and other details. The captain smiled quietly and passed the book around among the pilots when Joshua was on deck. The boy was so likable, so eager, so earnest, that a little make-believe in the bookkeeping could do no harm. Besides, the captain was curious to see what he would set down next.

"That boy's precocious," he said one day to Harry Dodge as they stood together on the after deck.

"Pre—*what?*" Harry demanded immediately. "He's all right, if that's what you mean."

The captain smiled at Harry's quick defense of the boy. "Precocious," he repeated. "Ahead of his years."

"Oh, aye, he's that, all right. He don't push himself, an' he don't argy, but he shore does ask some tough questions."

"I told his father I'd give him all the training he rated, and it looks to me like he rates the best I can give him. Help him when you can, Harry."

"Aye," said Harry readily. "I'll help him. He's wuth it."

At the moment of this conversation the pilot boat was hove-to off the capes. Joshua was in the cabin where he spent fully half his waking time now, hard at work on a lesson in arithmetic. Fifteen months earlier, at the age of ten, he had informed his parents with conviction that he had completed his education because "I write a good hand and perfectly understand arithmetic." He had not been long aboard the *Gallant Mary,* however, before Captain Chilton had drawn him into conversation on navigation. How did a captain find his way across the trackless sea, for weeks out of sight of land, "and sail right into the very spit-and-center of the harbor he had set out for?"

"Well, it takes arithmetic, don't it, sir?"

"It takes higher mathematics than you get under the head of arithmetic, boy."

"What more could there be?" Joshua asked, astonished.

"Like to know, would you?"

"Indeed, sir, I learned all the master had to teach, but my father said he was a backwoods ignoramous, and if it takes more to navigate a ship, I will have to know it."

"Would you work for it? Study hard, day after day for months on end?"

"If I need it to navigate, I would."

"You'll need it."

Joshua had felt sadly rocked back on his heels to learn
of such vast fields of mathematics as yet unguessed by him,
but there was no question in his mind that he must know
whatever would be needed for navigation. And so, hove-to
or jogging under reefed jib and mainsail, or moored in
Willoughby Bay, he went back to the school work he
thought he had finished. Mathematics, however, was only
one of the subjects the captain set him to studying. Driven
by an insatiable curiosity, he asked innumerable questions
about seafaring, and he was willing to go to any amount
of hard work to get the answers. Captain Chilton used
that driving curiosity to set him to studying ships—their
design, their rigging, the theory of sailing.

"Why does she come right into the wind if you let go of
the tiller, sir?" he asked one day in January.

"Ever notice the weather vane on your father's barn,
Joshua?"

"Yes, sir. Why, indeed, it does the same, doesn't it?"

"Know why?"

"Of course. It's set on a pivot, and the feather end catches
more wind, being wider than the point."

"Right you are, boy. And this vessel is pivoted, too, or
as good as. If she is lying along the pier, and you push one
end or t'other with an oar, say, that end goes off, doesn't it?"

"Yes, sir."

"But there is one point amidships, where, if you push her,
she'll move sideways. You can call that point her pivot
point. Now the pattern of her sails has a center, too, and if
you are good enough at your mathematics, you can find
it by measurements and calculations. A marine architect

has got to find it on his paper plans, before ever his plans go to the mold loft. He has got to step his masts so that the center of the wind's pressure on his sails will fall just a little abaft that pivot point of her hull in the water. Then she tends to pivot around that point and head into the wind. If the center of the wind's pressure comes forward of that pivot point, you will have to hold her up to the wind with her tiller. Such a vessel is no good for sailing close-hauled."

January passed into February, February into March. Sudden gales swept the bay and drenched the crew with spray, but the bite had left the wind. Spring was coming. Spring came, and Joshua worked on with unflagging zeal. Summer came and passed, and the winds grew cold again, and the boy's interest never wavered. Evidently he was one of those rare individuals who finds himself very early in the unyielding grip of a talent so demanding that it rules his whole life.

CHAPTER THREE

THE YEAR 1772 WAS ALREADY FIFTEEN MINUTES OLD. FRANCES Barney, believing that the mother of fourteen children was entitled to sit out a dance now and then, sank into one of the chairs that had been pushed back against the wall and watched the gyrations of her guests.

The reel ended, and Joshua came and stood at her side. She slipped an arm around him and held him tight.

"My little Joshua!" she said, smiling up at him. "How you have grown this past year! My big Joshua, I'll have to call you. And Captain Chilton says you are competent to navigate a ship anywhere!"

Joshua smiled indulgently. He wondered how often she had said the same thing these last few days. It amused him that she should take such pride in his progress, after her bitter opposition.

" 'Tis vastly comforting to know that you will be with Thomas," she said. "He is so careful, I know he will not let you run any risks, and you are so bold and daring."

After a year on the Chesapeake Joshua had been apprenticed to Captain Thomas Drysdale, husband of his sister Peg. Joshua knew that his mother expected Thomas to keep a sharp eye on him to see that he performed no dan-

35

gerous duties, and he devoutly hoped that the captain would do nothing of the sort. Amid the brilliant-hued raiment of the other men, the serviceable, snuff-colored suit the captain wore was conspicuous as he downed his drink before the fire. In turning to set his empty glass upon the mantel shelf, he saw through the crowd that Joshua and his mother were looking at him.

"Talking about me, Mother Barney?" he asked, coming toward them with his sailor's rolling gait. He was a man of medium height, with sandy hair, pale blue eyes set close together, a thin, tight-lipped mouth and a weather-beaten face.

"I was just saying that I am sure you will take good care of my boy, Thomas," she said.

"Trust me for that, Mother Barney. He'll be as safe as a church with me." Without another word he turned and stepped outside the front door, closing it after him, for the night was cold. A few minutes later he returned, and said to William Barney, "The night is clear, with a fresh breeze out of the north. I think it will veer westerly by dawn. Favorable for getting down the river on the tide. I'd thank you to send me and Joshua to my vessel, sir, so we can get a few winks before we sail."

William called for horses. Farewells were said in the hall, and all over again on the wide porch, in spite of the icy wind, with Joshua trying to be very dignified through it all. It was embarrassing, but a man had to make allowances for the sentimental ways of women. It seemed to the boy that he would never get away, but they were off at last, his cheeks wet with his mother's tears.

The raw little boom town of Baltimore was famous for the mud of its streets, but now they were frozen, and the horses stepped warily over the iron-hard ruts. The captain drew rein at the pier off which his vessel was anchored, and Joshua stopped beside him. Baltimore had two piers that had seemed a wonder of their day when a gentleman with the name of John Smith had built them in the year of Joshua's birth. They were each a thousand feet long, and they stood like huge, petrified marsh centipedes, their tails at Water Street, their heads nibbling at the ships that came into the harbor, their feet in mud and shallow water. Known as the East Pier and the West Pier, they had greatly increased the importance of Baltimore as a port, for fairly large vessels could tie up to them, even at low tide.

The captain dismounted and Joshua did likewise, and they handed their reins to the shivering servant who had ridden in behind them to return with the horses. Joshua stood with the captain, awaiting his orders. He had not long to wait.

"Get Mr. Wallace out of that tavern," he said in a peremptory voice Joshua had not heard before. "Tell him I say to round up any of the crew that's still ashore. We sail on the turn of the tide."

"Aye, aye, sir," said Joshua, immediately guessing that his relations with his brother-in-law would bear little resemblance to the very pleasant and profitable relations he'd had with Captain Chilton.

"And if you want to sail with me," Captain Drysdale continued, "just forget you're any sort of kin to my wife. Now bear a hand."

"I could easier forget you are any sort of relation to Peg, sir," Joshua said in his pleasantest voice.

The captain had already started for the pier, but at that he wheeled about. "Have I got to take a rope's end to you for insolence before we so much as up-anchor?" he demanded angrily.

"Not at all, sir. 'Tis just that Peg's been my sister so much longer than she's been your wife."

"Well, watch your tongue," the captain said tentatively, as if he had not yet decided against that rope's end. "Back talk I'll not tolerate."

"Aye, aye, sir."

Joshua had been working on the loading of the ship for several days, and he had been living aboard. He had been deeply humiliated to learn that he, a seaman with a year's experience on the Chesapeake, was not to sleep in the forecastle with the other sailors. Along with another apprentice he slept in the steerage amid a great mass of ship's supplies—coils of rope, spare sails, lumber, pitch, oakum, bales of old rope to be unravelled to make rope yarns, spun yarns and seizings, and all the other supplies that were needed to replace the ravages of service and keep the brig shipshape through long, stormy voyages.

Because of the hazard of fire in the midst of all those highly inflammable stores, the apprentices were allowed no light and so, after nightfall, must find their way in and out, and must dress and undress, in total darkness.

In this misery Joshua had as companion a country boy named Amos Gookin who had run away from a tyrannical father. He was not very bright, he had no ambition, and he had never felt the mystery and the romance of the sea but had chosen it as the surest way of putting himself beyond his father's reach. It had not occurred to him that the sea might prove to be a far greater tyrant than his father had ever been.

Joshua, after his year on the Chesapeake, felt vastly superior to Amos in spite of a difference of several years in their ages, and he resented being rated with such a lubber.

On this New Year's night—or morning—Amos was already asleep when Joshua came aboard, and the steerage was as dark as a coal mine. He set a course for the bed that he and Amos had rigged out of bales of oakum, for there were no such bunks in the steerage as the sailors had in the forecastle. He took off his shore clothes and laid them on a coil of rope by touch. He turned back the covers and crept in beside the sleeping Amos, grateful for the warmth of another body. A land lubber might have thought the oakum was hard, but it was much warmer than a hammock would have been. Besides, Amos had no blankets of his own and he would have been in a desperate plight if Joshua had not contrived a bed in which his own warm, homemade quilts could cover both of them. It really was a good bed for two robust, hard-muscled boys and the covers had scarcely been drawn to his chin before he had dropped into the deep, untroubled sleep of the healthy young animal that he was.

It seemed, though, that he had scarcely closed his eyes when he was roused by the beating of a huge bass drum. The mate was whaling the hatch cover so hard with a calloused palm that he produced a booming reverberation in the steerage. The booming ceased and his voice roared, "All hands! Bear a hand, you lubbers! All hands to make sail!"

A ship's crew is divided into two watches, or as a land lubber would call them, two teams; the larboard watch and the starboard watch. The larboard watch is commanded by the first mate who, however, is never called first mate but merely the mate. The starboard watch is commanded by the second mate; and for the ordinary routine of sailing, each watch is on duty for four hours and then off duty for four hours. Ship's time is measured by these four-hour watches and is marked off in half-hour intervals so that eight bells occurs at noon, at four o'clock, at eight, at midnight, and so on, right around the twenty-four hours; and each four-hour watch has its own name. The odd-numbered bells mark the half-hours.

To get under weigh from an anchorage, however, requires so much work that all hands must turn out. When Joshua was thus aroused at dawn by the command "All hands to make sail," he had slept barely three hours and at first he was too sleepy to feel the excitement of his first ocean voyage. He drew a deep breath, threw back the covers, yawned prodigiously, and swung his feet to the deck.

The whole ship was stirring into life. Joshua heard the muffled sounds of other feet, already booted, thumping on the deck, voices beyond bulkheads, the creaks and groans of the ship's timbers. Close beside him, Amos blundered about in the darkness. Unlike Joshua, he had gone to bed soon after dark and now he was bubbling with an exasperating lot of silly chatter.

"He hit that bell two times," he said. "I don't see no sense to hittin' it two times when it's five o'clock."

Joshua had explained the system of ship's bells to Amos so thoroughly that he was disgusted by his failure to understand, so he ignored him and concentrated on the business of dressing in total darkness. But Amos was wide awake, and he wanted to talk. "Five o'clock. Time for me to be a-milkin'."

"You lubber!" Joshua snorted. "Why didn't you stay with your cows and your pigs and your manure?"

Amos was delighted with that response. He snickered and went on with his chatter. Joshua's occasional flashes of temper never disturbed him, for there was no meanness in them. They were very different from his father's savage anger, and they never lasted long. As usual, Joshua was dressed first. "Stow the gabble," he said, "and come along." He was beginning to feel the excitement of his first ocean voyage, and he was impatient to go on deck; but if he went alone, Amos would be in trouble for being slow by contrast, so he waited; then felt his way cautiously between bales and crates to the ladder. Amos trailed behind, still chattering.

On deck the cold dawn wind in his face roused Joshua completely and excitement tingled in his veins. Amos shivered.

"Man the capstan!" Captain Drysdale roared. "Mr. Wallace, fore and main topsails, ready to sheet home!"

The crew had scarcely hit their bunks after their New Year's celebrations ashore and most of them were still groggy. Orders ran briskly from lip to lip, roared out by the captain and repeated by the mate, filling the cold air; but their execution was lubberly and the captain was exasperated. Blocks creaked, but they didn't creak loud enough. Men crept up ratlines when they should have raced aloft. They swayed drunkenly, or they sidled cautiously, out upon the footropes; and it looked as if a few of them would certainly drop like overripe apples. The captain bawled at them in rising anger. Sluggishly the sails broke out and slatted in the wind.

A pale dawn crept up the sky, and revealed two other vessels at anchor in the harbor. It grew brighter, and the field of vision took in the frost-nipped rushes that lined the river's shores, and the stakes that marked the channel.

"Hove short!" shouted Mr. Wallace from the bow, where he had been watching the anchor cable.

"Heave away!" roared the captain impatiently. "Sheet home, Mr. Wallace!"

Sails filled and strained at their sheets. The brig heeled and eased ahead. Little harbor waves slapped at her bluff bows. Her speed increased. She swung east, and then a little south of east. She left the harbor with a rush. The flat, grassy shore lines of the river seemed very near, and Mr. Wallace still stood in the bow to watch for the channel stakes and call orders to the helmsman.

"Come on, Josh-u-ay," said Amos, shivering. "Everybody's a-goin' downstairs."

"Go ahead, Amos. Go nurse your little pigs. I'll stay in the top to overhaul the rigging and light the sail out. Just one man to a top for that."

"Lordy, Josh-u-ay, whereat did you larn all that stuff? You said on that there pilot boat you didn't never have to climb up no masts."

"We had blue-water sailors, though, and I pumped 'em dry. You better get below, or Mr. Wallace will tan your hide for sogerin'." But Amos, instead of dropping swiftly down a stay, crept cautiously and clumsily down the ratlines, and Mr. Wallace bawled him out for a lubber.

Joshua wanted passionately to remain aloft, for to his mind nothing so clearly distinguished the noble calling of the sailor as his agility and hardihood in the rigging far above the heads of ordinary mortals. And, on this morning of all mornings, the *Nancy Anne* would be passing the mouth of Bear Creek about the time the sun peered above the Patapsco dead ahead, and he would see the family out on the point to wave him farewell as he stood on a foot rope far above the deck.

From his lordly height, in the pale light before sunrise, he looked down upon the deck and saw Amos, armed with bucket and mop, go to work in the tiny sty, built on the deck well aft, where three little pigs for the captain's table would be fattened on the ship's garbage. The farm boy, already homesick, had adopted them as his own responsibility for they were the one friendly, familiar detail in an alien world, and as far as the sailors were concerned, he was welcome to the most menial job on the ship.

"On deck, here, Barney!" Mr. Wallace called; and when the brig passed Bear Creek the boy was on his hands and knees, hard at work swabbing down the deck, dirty, icy water swirling all about him.

CHAPTER FOUR

"BARNEY," SAID MR. WALLACE ONE GUSTY MORNING, "THE captain says you are to hand out the daily rations to the cook. I'll show you how to keep the record in his book."

This was a job the captain had been doing himself, and he was very exact about it. He was known in the forecastle as a tight man with food. Joshua wondered mightily, but he need not have done so. It was in perfect keeping with the captain's character, and was just the first step in a policy designed to wring the last penny's worth of service out of a smart young apprentice.

When the boy found that his new duty required him to do a certain amount of paper work every day in the cabin, at the very same table on which the mate worked out the navigation, he was well pleased. He couldn't see any connection between the simple record of sea biscuit and salt horse consumed each day, and the brig's position at sea, but he was pleased nevertheless. It was Amos who grumbled, for Joshua's work in the cabin left him alone in the cold, dark steerage during much of his watch below.

As the *Nancy Anne* plowed her way eastward and north-ward across the wintry Atlantic, she often ran into head winds that blew her off her course and delayed her for days at a time, and Joshua got more than enough of the activity he had missed aboard the *Gallant Mary*.

As they made more northing, the days grew shorter— eight hours of a dull gray light and sixteen hours of total dark. Behind that unbroken pall of leaden clouds the blue sky had disappeared as if for all time. The sea, with no sunlight to strike down into it, was neither blue nor green nor gray but a glassy black, streaked everywhere with the white lace left by the hissing crests. A wild black and white sea under a dead gray pall of clouds—there were no other colors.

On any other ship, apprentices would have been kept at work on the deck, for there was plenty of work hauling at braces and halliards and sheets; but from the first, Joshua had shown such a fierce determination to go aloft at every opportunity that the captain had concluded it would take some of the conceit out of him to let him get one good scare; so he ordered the mate to let him go. Mr. Wallace strongly disapproved, but he had no choice. And Joshua didn't scare easily. By the time the vessel had sailed down the Patapsco to the Chesapeake, Amos had already become Joshua's faithful follower. The fiery Joshua was born to lead, while Amos was a dull clod, with a great capacity for doglike devotion, who would follow a master even while his insides froze with terror. So when sail was to be shortened for a gale, or let out afterwards, Joshua continued to go aloft, and Amos, often whimpering in terror, followed close at his heels. And Joshua trained him. On those rare days when the weather was not at its worst and the work was fairly easy, the able seamen grinned and winked at each other as Joshua labored to make a sailor of the country lad. Amos was frightened aloft, and being frightened, he was clumsy and stupid. Joshua coaxed, encouraged and cajoled; sometimes he commanded; and occasionally he lost his temper and stormed. Amos did try. He tried hard to do anything the younger boy wanted done; but too often Joshua had to finish his own work and then turn-to and help Amos.

The captain kept a sharp eye on them, for he was a little worried by Joshua's refusal to be frightened. But he carefully concealed his concern for he had an exaggerated fear of showing favor to a member of his family; and he treated Joshua more harshly than he did anybody else.

Mr. Wallace also kept a sharp and anxious eye on the boys; and he made no secret of his anxiety, though he never actually put it into words to the captain after his first orders on the subject. "Them boys!" he would exclaim, shaking his head, and glancing at Captain Drysdale. Or, "Them little prentices!" But he gained no headway on that tack.

He made no secret of his admiration for the way Joshua trained Amos. "Them two prentices together mighty nigh make one good hand," he told the captain once. "Barney might be better without Gookin, but Gookin without Barney'd be less'n nothin' at all. They could tail onto lines, though, if I had 'em down on deck."

"Leave 'em be!" the captain commanded. "Keep 'em together."

The huge seas tossed the little vessel as if she were an autumn leaf. In spite of their tarred canvas suits, the sailors were often drenched to the skin by the foam-streaked water that poured in through the hawseholes and, often, right over the bows or the weather bulwark. Their clothes never quite dried out. The time came when they had

46

to sleep in damp underwear, and from that, their blankets became damp.

On the twenty-first of January they were sailing close-hauled on the larboard tack, and Captain Drysdale, pacing the quarter-deck on the weather side, kept his eyes on a very black and stormy-looking sky to the north. At the forward end of his beat he turned to his left, and at the after end he turned to his right, so that his eyes were never away from that sky and the wild sea under it—except occasionally when he stared speculatively at the sails, as if trying to estimate to the ounce how much more pressure they could endure. The brig was rolling her lee scuppers under, and at every roll her weather shrouds lay almost horizontal. Every line in her rigging vibrated in the wind like a mighty violin string attacked by the bow of a giant maniac. When she heeled to leeward, the wild orchestration sank to a wail. When she rolled back against the wind, it rose to a shriek.

Mr. Wallace, amidships, stood in the lee of the weather bulwark and divided his attention between the ship and his captain, as if he expected a command. Finally it came. Captain Drysdale halted at the forward limit of his pacing. "Mr. Wallace!" he shouted above the screaming of the rigging and the crash and roar of the rushing seas, "All hands to shorten sail!"

"Mr. Babson, all hands!" bawled Mr. Wallace before the captain had finished speaking.

For some time Mr. Babson had been standing right alongside the forecastle hatch, and at the captain's first word he shot the cover open and bawled into the forecastle.

The starboard watch poured out on deck.

The big lower sails, called courses, had been furled and

47

the sailors were mounting higher into the rigging when the storm hit them, bringing sleet with it. The sheets had been let fly, and the sails were flapping with sounds like cannon shots. The sea soon made up beyond anything Joshua had yet seen.

Work aloft in that gale was not for green hands, and Joshua dreaded it right down to the pit of his stomach and heartily wished Mr. Wallace would order him to remain on deck, but he would have felt eternally disgraced to have hesitated; and where he went, the faithful, dogged Amos was sure to follow.

The men stood on the footropes, leaning down over the big spars, grappling for the leaping reef points on the flapping sails. The heavy winter canvas was heavier for the rains that had never dried out of it. It was frozen and slippery. It bellied with the slack in the sheets, so that at times it flew up and hit the sailors in the face, and at other times it jerked down and snatched reef points from all but the stoutest fists.

In a caprice of the wind the sail slatted back against the mast. Joshua caught a glimpse of a great sea rising against the bow and spurting in two great torrents through the hawseholes. It was just beginning to break in a mighty waterfall over the bulwarks when the sail bellied out again and cut his view off sharp. He caught his breath in an ecstasy of mingled fear and delight.

Amos bawled in pure terror, "She's a-sinkin', Josh-u-ay! Oh, Ma, Ma!"

And in fact, from where they stood, unable to see abaft the foot of the mainmast, it did look as if the vessel were taking the final plunge, for the entire forward deck was a mass of writhing, white-streaked water.

"Tie your reef points, Amos! Tie 'em!" Joshua yelled as he returned furiously to his work: "She'll come up!" His voice rose in a shrill shout of pride in his vessel. "Watch her! There she comes! Watch her throw it off!"

As he spoke, the *Nancy Anne*'s bows rose from that great sea, broke through the surface, and tossed her long jib boom defiantly at the clouds, while tons of water poured down her deck and spouted from all her scuppers.

White and shaken, Amos fumbled futilely at the last reef point until Joshua pushed him aside and tied it for him. When finally they got down on deck they were late for their dinner. They got their tin teapots and kids, and went to the galley, which was in the forecastle, and the cook served their portions. Being apprentices, they were forbidden to eat in the forecastle. Joshua watched his chance and made his start for the steerage, Amos at his heels, but he had miscalculated. A great sea boarded the brig, swept down upon the boys, picked them up and whirled them aft, leaving them stranded under the captain's gig as the water spread over the deck and poured away through the scuppers. They still clung to their tin teapots and kids, but the teapots were full of salt water and the kids were empty. Scrambling to their feet they dived into the steerage and slammed the hatch cover behind them.

"You save anything?" Amos asked.

"What do you think, stupid?" Joshua retorted. He stood on the first rung of the ladder and cracked the hatch cover to admit a narrow shaft of the gray light. Then, shivering, the two boys changed into dry clothes; or rather, into clothes that were somewhat less wet.

"Time for me to see about the rations," Joshua said

then. "Maybe I can get a few sea biscuits." He went off up the ladder and slammed the hatch cover tight behind him, while Amos crawled under the covers. Half an hour later Joshua returned, and, as usual, he left a crack in the hatch for light. Sometimes Amos complained that such a crack let in too much air, but Joshua always replied that it also let out some of the stink that came up from the bilges, and generally Amos said no more.

"I couldn't put tea in my pockets," Joshua said now, as he brought forth sea biscuits and counted them into two even lots. Amos accepted his share as a matter of course, and together they thumped them on the head of a cask to knock out the weevils. Then they munched slowly, for with no tea to dunk them in, eating sea biscuits was slow, jaw-breaking work. Aloft, the wind screamed in the rigging; against the single wall of planking the mighty seas lashed and thudded; the laboring ship creaked and groaned in all her joints; but the crackling of sea biscuits crunched between strong young teeth sounded like beef bones being chewed by hungry dogs.

For forty-eight hours the brig scudded before the gale; then the wind moderated, the clouds blew away, and the captain took a noon observation on the sun. When Joshua went aft with the report of the rations issued that day he found the mate swearing over figures that would not balance. If he could make his latitude obtained by dead reckoning check fairly well with that obtained from the captain's solar observation, he could feel reasonably sure of his longitude also; but his figures did not check. He swore with deep feeling, and sat biting his thumb. Joshua dallied over his own simple figures, studying the mate's figures upside down as he did so. The mate's result was 30° 27' W. longitude, much too good to be true.

"I'd be glad to check those figures for you, sir," Joshua offered, "if you have more important work on deck."

"*You* check 'em!" Anger flamed suddenly in the mate's face. Plainly he didn't believe the boy for a minute. "Yes, sir," Joshua hurried to say. "I can take observations and figure our position. Captain Chilton taught me, aboard the *Gallant Mary*."

The mate's face was hard with anger, and the boy felt his eyes, sharp as gimlets, seeming to drill holes in his skull; but Mr. Wallace was a fair man and as a rule he was good-tempered. Joshua met his searching scrutiny with a steady gaze; plainly he believed in himself. It seemed to him a long time before Mr. Wallace finally said, "You better make good your braggin', or I'll make it hot for you. I got no use for smart alecks."

"I can do it, sir. Just try me."

"Don't you touch my figures, though. Tear a page out of your galley record book. I'll be back inside half an hour," and he went out, evidently doubtful but still determined to be fair. He was back well within the promised half hour.

"Forty-three degrees, thirty-eight minutes, sir," Joshua told him.

"H-m-m-m-m-m," was all the mate said while he ran his eyes swiftly over Joshua's figures. "Sounds just about right, accordin' to my dead reckonin'. Did you check that, too, Barney?"

"Yes, sir. I checked everything." He showed Mr. Wallace a simple error in addition of angles that had caused all the trouble.

The mate went carefully over the figures again.

"Right to a minute, boy," he said, astonished. "How old are you, Barney?"

"How old would you say I am, sir?" Joshua parried, hating his youth and drawing himself up to his full height —which was not great.

"You don't look a day over fifteen to me."

"No, sir. I am not. You are a good judge of men, sir. I was just wondering if you would like me to check your figures every day. It would leave you free for more important work on deck, sir."

Mr. Wallace burst out laughing. There was nothing more important than navigation, and he knew that Joshua knew it. "Plan to walk your own quarter-deck some day, do you, Barney?"

"I hope to, sir," Joshua replied, his dark eyes snapping and his pleasure showing plainly in his face. He was not a handsome boy, but he was good to look at, with his beguiling, friendly glances and his air of competence.

"Well," said the mate thoughtfully, "you know Captain Drysdale. He don't want the crew to think he's favoring you for family reasons. You were sort of going to school aboard the *Gallant Mary,* though, warn't you?"

"Yes, sir."

"Well, I might put it to him that you'd like to continue your schooling under me. After all, an apprentice is entitled to instruction. You leave it to me, Barney. I'll see what I can do."

For several days the mate was short and sharp with Joshua, as if he had changed his mind entirely, or perhaps feared he had been too friendly for good discipline; and the boy was worried. That came to an end, however, one day when Mr. Wallace called him as he went off duty.

"Like to check our position?" he asked. "On your own time, mind," he added sharply, his brows drawn down just enough to make his eyes look hard and put the apprentice on notice not to take liberties.

Every day after that Barney either computed the position, with Mr. Wallace carefully checking his figures, or else he checked Mr. Wallace's computation. Blown about by the gales, sometimes off her course for several days as the little vessel was, navigation was a real problem, and dead reckoning was their chief reliance. There was great play for skill and judgment, and much discussion between captain and mate. Joshua listened eagerly, saying never a word and pretending to be hard at work on his own figures lest the captain chase him out of the cabin.

The days ran into weeks, and Amos grumbled and complained because Joshua was so seldom in the steerage during the daylight hours. He had come to hate the sea. He grew miserable and sullen, no longer accepting hardship with the good grace he had shown for a time. He snivelled and whined. Joshua tried hard to keep him in good spirits but it was a thankless task. "I'm a-goin' home when I git back," Amos said one day. "You can have yo' ol' sea, Joshu-ay. I've done got me a belly full of it. I don't keer how mean my ol' paw is, I'd ruther be home right now, an' him a-larrupin' me. Oncet I git home, I ain't never goin' on no boat, no more, no where, never!"

Not even the North Atlantic at its winter worst is without a break, and a morning came when no seas boarded the brig. When Joshua and Amos finished their watch at noon and took their dinners down to the steerage, Joshua left the hatch cover slid halfway open. A blast of icy air blew down upon them, and Amos shivered and complained as he gobbled.

"Oh, shut up, Amos!" Joshua snapped, his patience worn thin. " 'Tis no colder than with it shut, and this way we can see to eat, and besides it blows out the stink of that old bilge water."

Amos sucked up his hot tea noisily. He made a pig snout of his half-scalded lips and sucked cold air to ease them, while tears popped out of his vague blue eyes. "That ol' bilge water stink ain't bad. I don't mind it. It's like Paw's ol' pig sty back home."

"I mind it," said Joshua. " 'Specially when I'm eating."

The hatch stayed open, and the icy blast eddied into every corner and chased out some of the nauseating odor. And along with the blast came a shaft of dull gray light that made shadows in the corners and revealed, among other things, the apprentices' two spare suits of woolen underwear where they hung on pegs on the forward bulkhead, swaying with the motion of the ship and scraping and bumping lightly as they swayed, for they were frozen hard.

"We've got to get those things dried out," Joshua said.

"How kin you, Josh-u-ay?" Amos's nasal voice was plaintive.

" 'Tis time for me to see Doc about the rations. I'll take 'em with me."

He bundled the two suits—Amos's and his own—under his left arm and went up the ladder, using only his right hand for climbing. The drawers stood out rigidly fore and aft, and they felt as bulky as an armful of firewood.

On deck Mr. Babson promptly hailed him from aloft, where he was making the most of the milder weather to oversee the winding of some chafing gear, and he was profanely ordered to return those things to the steerage and leave them there until such time as all the sailors' things were well dried.

Fuming, Joshua returned down the ladder and flung the woolens down on the steerage deck. He made some sage remarks about able seamen and second mates in general and Mr. Babson in particular, and then he fell to work trampling hard on a pair of drawers. "Come on, Amos," he commanded. "Trample 'em flat. There's more'n one way to skin a second mate."

Obedient but without understanding, Amos proceeded to trample. When Joshua was satisfied that the garments were as flat as could be, he took off his tarred canvas jacket. "Wrap 'em around me," he said.

Together they wrapped and pummelled and pummelled and wrapped, until undershirts and drawers were wound snug and tight around Joshua's hard waist. Suppose he did look a little bulky amidships? In such weather, could anybody wonder that an apprentice wore extra-heavy clothes?

This time he made it safely to the forecastle, where the galley was; and luckily he found the weary larboard watch busy catching up on the sleep that three solid weeks of very foul weather had cost them—and snoring lustily in many fashions and many keys. Doc dozed on his stool in a corner, his head and shoulders cushioned by the undershirts and drawers that hung steaming before the galley fire. As Joshua came down the ladder, Doc opened his eyes.

"Did Mr. Babson put a crimp in yo' plans a mite ago?" he asked. "Or did I jes' dream I heard him beller at you?"

"He just thought he did," Joshua said with a broad grin as he opened his jacket.

"My lungs an' liver!" Doc's voice was a cautious rumble lest he wake one of the sleepers. "B'y, do ye know what them sleepin' beauties would do to me if they ketched me dryin' prentices' things ahead of theirn?"

Doc was a big fellow with a wide, good-natured mouth and gray eyes that looked sleepy but missed nothing. His mighty arms and shoulders had been developed by many a year in a northern lumber camp before his heavy fist had cracked a skull in a brawl and he had sought security at sea.

"Phooey!" Joshua snorted with equal caution. "Every one of 'em's scared to death of you, Doc!"

"B'y, if Mr. Babson gets wind of this, I'll fry yo' ears an' make you eat 'em." He scowled ferociously.

Joshua grinned happily. "They might taste better than salt horse for a change," he said, and proceeded to unwind the woolies, while Doc chuckled softly in his corner.

Late that afternoon it began to storm again. Under dense black clouds darkness came early, the sea made up under the gale, and two men were busy with axes, chopping off the ice that formed as fast as they could hack it away. Soon came sleet that cut men's faces and sheeted all the rigging with ice. Sail had to be taken in, and the oldest sailors dreaded it. Apprentices should have been kept on deck, but Joshua would risk anything rather than claim the privilege of tender years, and where he went, the faithful Amos, sick with fear, followed doggedly.

It was a nightmare job. The driving sleet cut cruelly, and when a man bent over a spar, his tarred canvas hat shielded his face only to let the sleet drive down the flaring neck of his ill-fitting canvas jacket. The reef points were like iron rods, and in bending them to strip the ice, the frozen fibers jabbed their fingers savagely. They scarcely realized this at the time, though, because of the numbness of their hands.

The sails jerked and slatted and banged, and reefing was a long, slow job.

"I am awful cold, Josh-u-ay!" Amos wailed once.

"Stow that gab and tie your reef points!" Joshua bawled back at him. "Who isn't cold? Tie those reef points so we can get down from here!"

Amos was quiet. The mast swung in mad arcs like a huge metronome. When the ship rolled down to starboard, Joshua was flung far out over the tortured sea with nothing between but the footrope and his own desperate grip on the ice-glazed spar. Black seas, flaming with the inner fire of phosphorescence, leaped to meet him and rushed swiftly past, and it seemed that the spar would certainly plunge him into them before it halted. When it did halt, it started the return arc with a sudden violence that seemed deliberately calculated to fling him off. He knew that if he did fall into those seething, ice-cold, black seas, they would devour him in a moment. Indeed, no effort at rescue would be made. So, at the limit of the roll, he stopped tying reef points and merely clung for his life. Every sailor aloft was doing the same.

Amos spoke again, but his voice was so weak Joshua did not catch his words. He was exasperated with the lubber, anyway. He was no good at all. He should have stayed at his milking.

The ship rolled far down to starboard. Amos banged Joshua's left shoulder, almost knocking him from the yard. He slid behind Joshua.

"Hold on, Amos!" Joshua's voice rose in a scream of

desperation and he let go the spar with one arm to grab for Amos. The icy timber was rushing back through space as the ship reversed her roll, whirling Joshua along with it. His right arm clamped the spar; his right fist was closed desperately on a reef point, while his left hand groped frantically for Amos. Amos's hands slid over Joshua's shoulder and down his sleeve. On ice-glazed clothing, neither could get a grip.

Joshua was alone on the spar. A piercing wail rose for a brief instant above the scream of the rigging, was choked off short.

"Man overboard!" Joshua cried again and again, knowing as he did how futile it was.

The spar swung in its dizzy arcs. The brig drove on through the night and the storm. Tears froze on Joshua's cheeks, and sobs choked him. Blindly, mechanically, under the compulsion of habit and the need of the whole organism for survival, he finished his job, and with the other sailors he climbed cautiously down the ice-sheeted ratlines to the deck.

CHAPTER FIVE

JOSHUA MISSED AMOS BITTERLY. HE EVEN MISSED HIS GRUM-
bling and complaining. He reproached himself for letting
such a lubber go aloft, though he never once thought of
the captain's responsibility for both apprentices, or of his
assurance to Mother Barney—"He'll be as safe as a church
with me." He felt only relief when Mr. Wallace ordered
him to remain on the deck for the rest of the voyage. The
steerage had become unbearably lonely, and he used all
his ingenuity to keep busy and remain out of it as long
as he could. He dawdled over his calculations in the cabin;
he strung out his conferences with Doc over the rations
until the imperative demand for sleep finally drove him
below. In that bleak solitude, with no work of any sort
to absorb his attention, tears stung his eyes, and he dashed
them angrily away with the back of a tarry fist; for tears
were a womanly weakness and he hated them. Life in
the steerage had become almost unbearable and when
the *Nancy Anne* finally sailed into the harbor of Liverpool
he was in a state of deep depression.

His nature was normally bouyant, however, and the
variety and quantity of shipping in that great port soon

diverted his thoughts, for Amos had not shared these scenes with him as he had shared the steerage. He had few duties, and he spent his free time wandering along the quays, looking at ships and talking to sailors; and it was doubtless pure luck that he was not shanghaied for service on some outbound ship.

These pleasant, carefree days were cut short, however, and in an unexpected manner. Captain Drysdale called him to the cabin one morning.

"The owners have sold the *Nancy Anne* right out from under me," he said. "You will take passage to Dublin and engage passage for the two of us to Baltimore on the first good vessel. Write me when she will sail, and where you lodge."

He counted out money. Joshua looked at his brother-in-law's cold, pale eyes, buttoned the money into an inside pocket, said "Aye, aye, sir"; listened stolidly to a lecture on the dangers of sharpers who were always on the look-out to separate a sailor from his money; said "Aye, aye, sir," again, and walked out. He was secretly uneasy over the responsibility of travelling alone in a foreign country with the harsh, penny-pinching captain's money in his pocket; but that was for him to know and anybody else to guess who could; it didn't show.

He went ashore and walked along the quay. The captain had given him no instructions about where or how to engage passage to Dublin, or where to lodge when he got there. A sailor told him that packet boats plied between the two cities as regularly as wind and tide would permit, and directed him to one that was to sail in about an hour. Joshua looked her over, but she was dirty and crowded.

By this time he had begun to feel that the responsibility for the captain's money was a small price to pay for a brief stretch of complete freedom from his cold calculating supervision. Aboard the *Nancy Anne* he had seldom spoken to Joshua and never in friendship, but it had been impossible to feel free of the scrutiny of those pale, cold eyes. A holiday mood came over the boy, and he determined to make this little voyage in a pleasanter manner than seemed possible on a crowded packet.

He strolled along the quays. To his right, ships from all the ports of the world were tied up, their immense jib booms sloping high over his head and spanning the entire width of the street. To his left, numberless drays rumbled and clattered over the cobbles. Sailors swarmed everywhere. He stopped to chat with many of them, and finally one of them pointed out a small vessel which, he said, would soon be sailing for Dublin. Joshua stood on the quay and looked her over critically. She was no larger than the *Gallant Mary,* and she had a dash and saucy grace that reminded him of that little vessel of pleasant memories, though she was cut on different lines. Her rigging was neat and trim and taut. Her hull was a bright and shining black, with a vivid green stripe along the run, and her deck was scrubbed clean—which was more than could be said for some he had seen. She was, in short, just the vessel to charm an exacting young seaman's eye.

A tall man with immense shoulders stood on her deck. Joshua stepped aboard and went up to him, and he turned on the boy with a truculent air.

"You are Captain O'Connell, I believe, sir?" Joshua said.

"And what if I am?" The tall man regarded Joshua with eyes narrowed to slits of intense blue.

"Barney is my name, Captain, and I'd like to talk a little business with you."

"Barney, is it? Well, me bould young Barney, 'tis not like them thievin' Englishmen that ye speak, an' 'tis plain to be seen that ye are no son of Erin. Ye sound to me like you might be from the Colonies."

"Right you are, Captain. From Baltimore in the Colony of Maryland."

"Baltimore, is it? I have heard the name. An' what is this little matter of business ye would speak of, Mr. Barney of Baltimore in the Colony of Maryland?"

"I was told you are just about to sail for Dublin. If you are, I'd like to engage passage with you."

"There's the packet boats for the likes of that."

"Aye. Tubs. Dirty, too. Dirty, wallowing tubs. Yours is the first vessel I've seen that I'd care to sail on. She's clean, she's well kept and shipshape, and she has the lines of a good, fast vessel."

"Ye don't say!" Captain O'Connell regarded the boy speculatively. "H-m-m-m. Have ye, by chance, been in God's own green isle?"

"Why, yes. We stopped in Cork to fill our water casks."

"Oho. At Coorrk, did ye say? An' did ye, by chance, go ashore?"

"I did."

"An' did ye, by chance, visit the foine castle o' Blarney that sits on a grand great hill beyant the ancient city o' Coorrk?"

"Why, no. Castle? No, I didn't see any castle."

Captain O'Connell continued to regard the boy quizzically for a moment. His face was grave. In fact, it was a face not easily read—tough, leathery, weathered, of an age impossible to guess, and yet, a genial face, with a faint suggestion of a smile lurking in the corners of the wide mouth. Joshua began to feel that he was being made the butt of some obscure joke, but he was not a sensitive lad, and his own frank, friendly smile flashed at the captain.

"All right, b'y," the captain said. "Ye've an honest face and a bould eye, and a civil tongue between yere teeth, and if the bloody Liverpool police are after ye, that ye dodge the packets, I'll swear 'tis nothing more than some gay lark with no harm to it at all at all. An' besides, I'd be glad of a chance to do thim in the eye anyway, for I have no love for the English."

The captain's notion tickled Barney immensely, and his gay, infectious laugh rang out. He left it at that. Feeling rather important at being mistaken for a fugitive from the law, he struck a bargain with the captain, and went off to the *Nancy Anne* for his sea chest.

Life aboard the *Bounding Betty* reminded Joshua of his year with Captain Chilton. There was little formality between Captain O'Connell and his crew of four, and only one cabin for all of them; and the yarns that were spun were a delight to listen to. Joshua even tried his hand at making up a few yarns of his own, just to prove that he wasn't entirely taken in by the tall tales the Irish sailors told; and the voyage proved to be all too short.

"Go to the Golden Herring Inn," Captain O'Connell told Joshua. "Tell Thomas Malloy ye're a friend o' mine.

And see Mr. Gilligan for passage to Maryland. See Thomas Malloy first. Ye can lodge with him, and he will direct ye to Mr. Gilligan."

Joshua found the Golden Herring by virtue of a large, carved fish on which a few faded patches of gilt still showed. He entered, and looked around him curiously. In front of him a small peat fire glowed red on the hearth, and meat was broiling on a spit. To the right was the tap room where Joshua discovered a squat, broad-shouldered man with a twisted, broken nose, black eyes, and a slit of a mouth. Certainly not a pleasant-looking individual.

"Are you Mr. Thomas Malloy?" Joshua asked him with some misgiving.

"Who wants to know?"

"Well, if you are, Captain O'Connell brought me from Liverpool aboard the *Bounding Betty*. He told me I could lodge with you, and I was to say I am a friend of his."

"Oh, aye," said the man, twisting his mouth into what was doubtless intended for a cordial smile. "Any friend of Captain O'Connell is a friend of mine. 'Tis welcome ye are, Mr. . . ."

"Barney, Mr. Malloy. Joshua Barney, of Maryland."

A merry, blue-eyed girl was serving a dinner to the men at the tables. "Will ye have yer dinner now, Mr. Barney?" she asked.

Joshua said that he would. While he ate, he asked Mr. Malloy where he could find Mr. Gilligan.

"Right here," said the landlord. "He comes in here every day for his dinner. He'll be here any minute now."

He had hardly spoken the words when the door flew open and in stamped a hogshead of a man, followed by a gust of winter wind.

"Food, Molly, food!" bellowed the newcomer. "Drink, Molly, me sweet little colleen! Food and drink!" His voice was a jovial bellow, and Mr. Malloy and Molly went into furious action. Molly rushed to the kitchen, while Mr. Malloy escorted him to Joshua's table.

"Set here, Mr. Gilligan, sir," he said. "Here's Mr. Barney, a decent young gintleman from the Colony of Maryland who is lookin' for ye to secure passage home. Captain O'Connell's friend, he is."

"Mr. Barney, 'tis a pleasure, sorr!" bellowed Mr. Gilligan. "We will eat first and we will talk business afterwards." He sat down opposite Joshua and drained his mug, returning it to the table with a crash that would have split anything short of solid oak. He smacked his lips, blew a mighty sigh of satisfaction, brought forth a heartfelt belch, wiped his mouth with a backhanded swipe of a black-bristled paw, and smiled at Joshua, showing a remarkably fine set of gleaming white teeth. His eyes were a merry blue, his hair a set of curly black bristles. His face was round and ruddy.

When Molly brought his dinner, Mr. Gilligan fell upon it like a starving bear. As he ate he launched into a dissertation on the virtues of Dublin, the iniquities of the English, and the opportunities afforded a young man for entertainment in so fair a city. He leaped from subject to subject and punctuated his remarks with lusty smackings of his lips, deep and hearty belches, and in spite of the flow of conversation, he managed to gobble a huge meal. When he had finished and shoved his plate from him with a satisfied sigh, he invited Joshua to his countinghouse, where they could talk business.

Joshua went, feeling that he was being swept along in

the wake of a genial tornado. He inspected a stout brig that was soon to sail for Baltimore, was well pleased with her, and engaged passage on the spot. He then sat down and wrote a letter to Captain Drysdale, which he left with Mr. Gilligan to be dispatched to Liverpool by the next packet.

His business attended to, he spent the afternoon strolling about the water front and the streets of the town; and he prudently returned to the Golden Herring before sundown. He was just thinking about eating when the door flew wide and Mr. Gilligan's huge form filled the doorway while his equally huge voice filled the low-ceilinged room. "Mr. Barney! Come up to supper wi' me. Come along! Don't set there gogglin'! Come along 'fore 'tis all et up!" And taking acceptance for granted, he turned and strode back across the street to the carriage that awaited him.

Joshua hurried after him. The carriage, he saw, had once been handsome, but now it was mud-spattered and shabby. A coachman and a footman perched aloft on the box. Their livery was as worn and shabby as the carriage, and they slumped in their seats like a pair of plow hands. The horses, though, to Joshua's untrained eye, appeared conspicuously fine—beautifully matched chestnuts, spirited and restless. He was scarcely seated before they were off at a fast clip.

The coachman straightened up and handled his lines and his whip with skill and pride. Mr. Gilligan talked steadily, interrupting himself frequently to shout greetings to people in the carriages they passed—for the Gilligan team was running a race with everything on the road.

In one gleaming, polished carriage, an austere-looking

gentleman rode alone. Mr. Gilligan did not shout at him, but tipped his hat with elaborate courtesy—and got an icy lift of the eyebrows for his trouble. "Gentry!" he explained in an awed tone. "The castle! I've got more money than him now, an' I made every blessed cent of it. Come right up out of a Dublin gutter, I did, too! Ye'd never guess it though, now would ye? But I had to go to the Colonies to do it—what with the strangle hold England's got on this country. Here, 'tis all a pore man can do to live."

The carriage sped up the long hill outside the town, past some beautiful estates. It turned into a country road, and finally through a handsome gateway into a private lane. The track between the wheel ruts was grown up in grass and weeds. Dead leaves and fallen branches from the stately trees of a fine grove littered the ground. The place was utterly unkept.

The coachman drew up with a flourish at a large, imposing stone house. Dogs greeted them, and out of the doorway and from various points in the spacious grounds a flock of black-haired, merry-faced urchins converged upon them. Mr. Gilligan bellowed at them and they piped merrily back at him, laughing gleefully and dancing around him. He swung the youngest to his shoulder, his hat was immediately knocked off, and he stamped indoors without a glance to see if it was recovered from the trampling young feet and the romping dogs. The din was deafening.

There was no such thing as an introduction. Mrs. Gilligan was a ruddy woman, her black hair streaked with gray. Her personality was overpowered by that of her husband. The house was spacious, sparsely furnished and shabby. The floors were bare and muddy. The family went at once to a dinner that was ready on a huge table in a huge room, where a turf fire glowed redly on the wide hearth. There must have been twenty people at the table; and three men, evidently neighbors, strolled in during the meal, drew up chairs, and were promptly supplied with plates and food. A dozen big platters of meats, fish and game were scattered about and service was catch-as-catch-can in spite of servants, whose principal duties seemed to be to refill empty platters and to enter without restraint into the political arguments that raged around the board. Joshua gathered the impression that about half the children present were Gilligans and the other half, neighbor children.

Mr. Gilligan made more noise than anybody else in the room, but he had plenty of competition and he seemed to miss little of what was said. Once, when eighteen-year-old Maggie confided to Joshua that she and all her brothers and sisters except the baby were Americans, her father interrupted himself in the middle of a sentence to bellow at her that she and her brothers and sisters were Irish like their mother and father, and that was something she'd do well to remember.

Scraps of food and well-picked bones were flung to the dogs all through the meal resulting in some lively scrimmages about the feet of the diners, but any dog so rash as to try to snatch food from a plate was sure to get his nose well rapped with the back of a knife blade.

Joshua was accustomed to a big family and plenty of guests, but to more order and to noiseless, well-trained servants, and at first he looked at this wild performance in amazement. Mrs. Gilligan ate placidly, however, and did her share of the talking, and Joshua soon decided it was the most diverting meal of his life and he resolved that when he grew up and had a large family he would run it the Gilligan way. He soon entered into the uproar with gusto.

When the dinner was over, the adults settled down to a quiet evening around the hearth. Four of them started a game of cards; others preferred to sit and talk. Those within Joshua's age range pushed the furniture back against the wall and started to dance. They danced well, and most of them seemed able to play the spinet, and took turns at it. Maggie, black-haired, blue-eyed, freckled and buxom, took charge of Joshua and set out to teach him their dances, but they were continually interrupted by the smaller fry zipping back and forth across the floor in a furious game of tag. This was so discouraging that Maggie finally gave up. "We can't dance with our feet bein' knocked out from under us every two minutes by a lot of dirty brats," she told Joshua.

When the guests began to leave, Joshua said that he would go also.

"Bring around the carriage!" Mr. Gilligan bellowed. Half a dozen youngsters raced to the servants' quarters with the order.

"Ye see how 'tis, Barney, b'y," Mr. Gilligan roared. "There's always extry places laid an' extry victuals for our friends. We'd be hurt did ye wait to be bid. Come up any day or every day an' eat wi' us 'til ye sail. 'Twill be a short time, at best."

"Yes, do," said Mrs. Gilligan with a cordiality that could not be doubted, and young Kathleen, who was just Joshua's age but fancied he was much older, said shyly, "Come tomorra, early. There's a pony to ride. We'll come to the inn for ye." Her heavy black curls clustered around a little monkey face sprinkled with freckles in which the startling Gilligan eyes, set well apart, sparkled brightly, and Joshua readily agreed.

As he left he saw the youngest Gilligan sound asleep on the bottom step of the stairway in the hall, his head resting on an outflung arm on the next step above. Mrs. Gilligan gathered him up and cushioned him on her ample bosom until Joshua was out the door.

CHAPTER SIX

IT WAS LATE IN MAY WHEN MR. GILLIGAN'S BRIG FINALLY sailed up the Patapsco River on a flood tide and made fast to Mr. Smith's East Pier. Captain Drysdale promptly ordered his apprentice to live with his family, since that would be cheaper than maintaining him in the town and there was no knowing when he would secure another command. Joshua had been away for nearly five months, so it was with soaring spirits that he hired a horse and set out at an impatient gallop for the Bear Creek Plantation.

His livery stable nag soon tired of that pace, and Joshua had time to savor the fragrance of the pines, and of fresh-turned earth, and he wondered that he had never noticed it before. He breathed deeply of it while his nag travelled at an easy lope; then, as he turned into the white oyster-shell lane of the plantation, he once more whipped up to a hard gallop. The flying hoofs beat a satisfactory tattoo on the hard lane, and he shouted and waved gaily to a crew of negro slaves working in one of the fields. They replied with cries of pleasure, flung down hoes and started on a run for the house. Nathan, the indentured white overseer, put his own horse into a gallop on a converging course. It's a race, Joshua thought, and gleefully accepted the challenge.

A gardener, working on the boxwood borders in front of the house, dropped his shears and ran to catch the bridle as Joshua reined in and sprang to the ground; but the boy was sadly disappointed in the black man's greeting.

Nathan came close behind him, sprang down, and flung his bridle also to the gardener. But he had no hilarious greeting. Instead, his face was grave as he took the offered hand in both of his. Joshua scrutinized that solemn face and uneasy questions sprang to his mind. As far back as he could remember, he and Nathan had been firm friends and Nathan was a cheerful man always. His indenture was almost complete, and he would soon be set up with a little farm of his own; so now his gravity was frightening.

"Bad news, Mr. Barney," he said. "Powerful bad."

"Bad news, Nathan?" Joshua repeated, at a loss for words.

"A terrible accident, lad. 'Tis your father. He ain't with us no more."

"Not . . . ?"

"He were a fine man, lad, and a kind master. None kinder. He'll be sore missed."

Joshua's stories of adventures were forgotten. His desire for the sea was quenched—at least, for a time. He was glad to be living at home with his family, for he wanted to spend every minute with them, as if the loss of one of them had made him suddenly more aware of his love for the others.

About noon of the day after his arrival a boy rode up

to the kitchen door and delivered a note addressed to Joshua. He opened it and read:

Joshua Barney, Apprenticed S'man:

Sir:

I am appointed to command the Ship *Sidney*, Mr. John Smith, owner. She lies at Whetstone Point, ready to take Cargo. You will return with bearer immediately and report to me at Counting House, Gay & Water Streets.

Thomas Drysdale, *Master*

Incredulous, Joshua read this brief, hard note over again. Why, the man was Peggy's husband! Peggy went to Baltimore yesterday to be with him! He knows! He just doesn't care!

Rage boiled in Joshua. He showed the note to his mother, and then, in such a storm of passion as she had never seen him show, he tore it to bits and flung the fragments on the floor. Then he stormed outside where he could vent his feelings in the good, round seamen's oaths he had been learning.

"But you'll have to go, son," his mother said when he returned. "You're articled to him, you know."

Angry and rebellious, Joshua repacked the things he had only yesterday unpacked, said a sad farewell, and set out on the return journey through the fields and forest.

In Baltimore he rode to Water and Gay Streets, where he tied his horse to the hitching rail outside Mr. Smith's counting house. When he entered, he found Captain Drysdale standing at a window, as if he had been watching the boy's approach. Without a word of greeting, or of regret for his loss, the captain gave his order.

"We're sailing soon's we can get her laden," he said.

"Get on down to Whetstone Point. Get aboard and tally her cargo in. And see the stevedores don't soger on the job. See Mr. Wilson, and tell him I sent you." He shoved a sheaf of invoices at Joshua. "Bear a hand," he said. In the language of the sea, "bear a hand" means "get a hump on you."

Without speaking, Joshua took the paper and stalked toward the door. Captain Drysdale promptly called him back. "Did you hear me speak to you?" he demanded in that cold, level voice Joshua hated.

"Aye, sir."

"I expect the proper answer."

"Aye, aye, sir."

"See you remember your manners. Now bear a hand."

Joshua mounted and rode on to Whetstone Point, which is about three miles down-river from Baltimore. As he approached the point, he saw the spars of a great ship towering above the trees, and he understood why she was being laden at Whetstone Point instead of her owner's own pier. Such a ship could not come into the harbor of Baltimore; she drew too much water.

When he rode out onto the cleared land at the tip of the point and beheld the ship at the pier, he saw she was truly a great ship. Even in his anger his quick eye noticed that she was rigged to carry skysails. In Liverpool he had heard of a skysail ship, but it was very new and this was the first he had seen. He tipped his head back to trace the lines of her slim, tall masts to their peaks. He climbed the gang plank and stepped onto her deck, and there he stood and looked about him.

He had seen other ships as large, though he had never before stepped aboard one. To his left was the raised

74

poop deck, and upon it, evidently, would be the quarter-deck. To his right was the raised forecastle, and there, he knew, the crew's quarters would be. Between the forecastle and the poop stretched the main deck, larger than the entire deck of the *Nancy Anne*.

This ship really was something to stir a young sailor's fancy, rage or no rage, and before looking up the mate, Joshua walked forward. The deck was littered with great coils of bright new rope, apparently for replacing all running rigging, for a few sailors were working aloft and the bright yellow strands rose snakily from their coils to the lofty spars.

After a few moments of inspection, Joshua turned aft. Two men were deep in conversation on the quarter-deck, and Joshua surmised that one of them must be the mate, since he wore the seaman's short jacket and the loose breeches, chopped off short just below the knee, while the other wore the neat, snugly-fitting breeches of the landsman. At the foot of the mainmast a one-eyed sailor with a long scar down the left side of his face from blind eye to jaw was busy paying out rope to other sailors working aloft. His tarred canvas hat sat jauntily on the back of his head, and his hair, a dingy gray at the temples, was drawn down smoothly into a well-tarred pigtail that lay on the nape of his neck. His face was deeply lined and he looked old for a sailor, but when Joshua came up to him he turned on the boy a single very bright blue eye.

"Where is Mr. Wilson?" Joshua asked him.

That one bright blue eye looked him over insolently, as if its owner doubted whether a boy was entitled to the information. Eventually he decided in Joshua's favor, though, for he jerked his head toward the poop deck.

"The black un," he said, his mouth twisting away from the scar in a lopsided grimace.

Joshua walked aft and mounted the ladder to the poop deck. "The black un," Mr. Wilson, was black of hair and deeply tanned. Extraordinarily heavy, bushy black eyebrows met above his high-bridged nose. His skin was weathered to a coarse, rough, leathery finish. A heavy black stubble of twenty-four hours' growth covered his cheeks almost to his eyes. He had a hard, aggressive appearance that would discourage any tendency to start trouble with him. His build was short, stocky and powerful, with muscles bulging under the shoulders of his brief, ill-fitting jacket and calves that were lumpy in his coarse black cotton stockings. A third person, seeing Joshua and the mate together for the first time, might easily have taken them for father and son, for they were much the same build and complexion; both had the same jaunty, reckless air, the same appearance of immense vitality and competence.

Joshua took in these details as he approached. Hairiest ape ever I clapped eyes on, was the way he summed him up.

It would be a breach of discipline for an apprentice to interrupt the mate on the sacred quarter-deck, but several factors conspired to betray Joshua into just that mistake. In the first place, the mere fact that he and Mr. Wallace had shared the vital responsibility of navigation over half the stormy North Atlantic had breached the wall that separates an apprentice from a mate. In the second place, Joshua was still in a fuming rage over his hardhearted captain. And finally, Mr. Wilson deliberately misled the the boy by his first words.

"And who may you be, young sir?" he asked, his voice

throttled down to a soft rumble that, even to Joshua's heedless mood, seemed oddly out of keeping with his piratical appearance.

"Joshua Barney, sir. Captain's apprentice."

"Oho, so you're the captain's apprentice, are you?" he said in the same deceptively soft rumble, looking the boy over from head to foot as he said it. "And just what might you want with me, Mr. Captain's Apprentice?"

"Captain's orders, sir. He said I was to report to you at once, and then tally in the cargo." He would have been wiser if he had said, "I was to report to you for your orders."

The mate's voice swelled suddenly to a profane roar of rage for the boy's thoughtless interruption of his conversation and he wound up by ordering Joshua out of his sight "before I lose my patience with ye, ye blighted captain's pet."

"Aye, sir," Joshua replied. He turned back to the main deck, outwardly calm but mentally dazed by Mr. Wilson's unreasonable rage. Evidently this mate was something wholly new in his brief experience. Plainly he was in for trouble, but he was so angry with the captain that the knowledge did not bother him then. He'd take care of that when he came to it.

When the *Sidney* passed the mouth of Bear Creek, Joshua was in the maintop, and he waved to the family assembled on the point to see him pass; but he didn't get the thrill from it that he would have on that first voyage aboard the *Nancy Anne*. The maintop was an old story to him now.

When the watch was relieved at noon, Joshua slid down

a stay and started for the forecastle with the rest of his watch, but Captain Drysdale called him to the poop deck. And there in the presence of the mate, and within the hearing of the helmsman, he told the boy he was to keep all the records of the cargo, post the log and check and correct all computations for navigation. All of these were the duties of the mate, and a competent mate would not need to have his figures checked, much less corrected; and least of all, by an apprentice. If Captain Drysdale had slapped Mr. Wilson across the mouth, that gentleman would have had no greater cause for resentment. He wheeled on the captain in amazement, only to see an indifferent back moving deliberately down the companion-way to the cabin. Joshua was left alone to face the outraged mate.

If the captain had said, "Mr. Wilson, I have a young apprentice who has shown a great aptitude for figures and I would consider it a favor if you'd work him in on the navigation and in all possible ways push him ahead; and to offset any trouble that may cause you, you may turn over to him the records of the cargo," the mate might have grumbled a little in his sleeve, but he could not have felt mortally insulted. Instead, the captain had used Joshua as the instrument of an unpardonable insult, and then had gone off and left him to face the mate's rage all alone.

By comparison, Joshua's own disregard of the mate's dignity that first day aboard was nothing. The boy tried desperately to think of something to say that might salve Mr. Wilson's outraged feelings, but he could not lay his tongue to a word; and indeed, he was given very little time. With the blood almost bursting from his face and neck, the mate roared out a terrific volley of profanity that wound up with the command to "get out of my sight!"

Joshua got. But just as he reached the forecastle hatch, another roar jerked him back to the quarter-deck on the run.

"So I am no longer able to perform my duties as a mate!" Mr. Wilson bellowed in tones that must have shaken the timbers of the captain's cabin. "So I must have the captain's pet always on my neck! Checking my figures! Correcting 'em! So we won't go aground on the North Pole, mayhap! Or the Cape of Good Hope! All right, blast your eyes! I'll skin any man alive that disobeys an order on this ship, and I'd be the last man to disobey a command of the captain! Get to work!" And with that, Mr. Wilson stamped off to the main deck, thereby frightening several sailors half out of their wits for fear he had seen their grins of delight over such a rare show. Joshua was left to start a job with only the vaguest idea as to how it should be done.

He watched the retreating back of the mate in deep consternation. They were still in the bay, and no navigation was to be computed, but there was a log to start and there were cargo records to be set up, neither of which Joshua had ever done. Well, he had better do something, so he went slowly down the companionway into the sacred precincts of those two high potentates, the captain and the mate.

He had never made an entry in the *Nancy Anne*'s log, though he had read it from start to finish and knew exactly how it was to be done; so he started the log of this voyage. However deliberate he might be over that, it required only a few minutes to copy the notes from the slate into the book. When that was done he got out the cargo manifests, spread them on the table, and sorted them according to commodity. What he should do with them, if anything, he really did not know. On the former voyage, Mr. Wallace had attended to it long before Joshua had been permitted to dispense the rations; and anything he did now could be repudiated by the mate. He had to do something, though, so he went slowly and cautiously to work. He added up the weights of the different commodities—wheat in one column, flour in another, and so forth. In like fashion he made a neat tabulation of their values. For three and a half hours that should have been his own time, he toiled, then he cleared the table and went into the forecastle in a seething temper. As he dropped down the ladder into that dimly-lit space, he heard a voice say in biting derision, "Well, mates, here comes the captain's pet," and he heard the delighted snickers of the other men of his own watch. If he let that pass, his life in the forecastle would be unbearable. If he had been in his usual sunny, happy frame of mind he might have found a way to handle the matter diplomatically. Instead, his temper directed him. "Scarface," he said, "I think you are the soger that called me the captain's pet."

"What's ut to ye?"

"When I hit, I want to be sure I hit the right man."

The old man was offended on two counts. The sailors called him Pop, and he hated being called Scarface; and *soger* is the most insulting word in the sailor's vocabulary. Joshua had called him both. "I said ut!" he retorted angrily. "I say ut again."

Pop had no idea that the boy would dare attack him, and he would not have taken it seriously if he had known it. He was the scarred veteran of countless savage fights, and the thought that a boy of thirteen could hurt him would have seemed fantastic. Joshua's lunge was so swift that it caught him completely off guard. He landed a left hook on Pop's one eye, and an upper cut to the chin, and when Pop's head snapped back, Joshua hit that eye again.

With a roar of rage Pop surged to his feet. He wasn't damaged by Joshua's blows; merely insulted—though that eye did hurt. He was heavier and taller and much stronger than Joshua, and on visible points he should have been able to reduce the boy to a mass of bleeding wreckage in a few minutes. But Joshua had some advantages that were real, though not obvious. He was incredibly fast, where Pop was slow. He had two good eyes for judging distances, whereas Pop's single eye misjudged distances. And Joshua had a savage, fighting heart that gloried in battle, once his blood was hot, and that rendered him insensible to pain; and he had a mind that grew cool and cunning and worked with uncanny speed as his blood grew hot. But these were things that neither Pop nor any of the other sailors knew, and the boy's performance during the next few minutes in the half-light of the forecastle was so astonishing that the other men drew back into their bunks to give the fighters a clear deck.

In the dim light Joshua was never exactly where he appeared to be. He didn't stand still for an instant. He moved with incredible speed. He watched for Pop's clumsy, roundhouse swings, and he darted in and darted out of reach, in a fashion that bewildered the slow-witted, slow-moving Pop. He landed galling blows that drove Pop to raging recklessness. Nearly half his blows were aimed

81

at that one eye, and most of them landed. And while no one of them had enough force to do much damage, enough such blows would surely close it entirely.

Pop used no strategy, and he didn't aim his blows. He simply swung from the shoulder, and Joshua's sharp eyes could see each flail-like blow getting started well ahead of time. In the backwoods school he had attended, fights were an almost daily occurrence and in that hard school he had been an apt pupil.

But in the confined quarters of the forecastle such a fight could not last long and finally one of those wild swings caught Joshua on the side of the head, sent him spinning, and laid him out cold. The sailors were so delighted with the boy's performance against heavy odds that they leaped out and surrounded him before Pop could finish him off in approved forecastle fashion—with his boots. While several of them held the raging Pop, two of them picked Joshua up, head and heels, and tossed him into his upper bunk as handily as if he had been a sack of wheat.

The next thing Joshua knew, and that but dimly as his mind cleared, he was floating on a sea of aches and pains that seemed concentrated in his arms, shoulders and head. During the heat of the battle he must have ignored many blows before that roundhouse swing to the side of his head had laid him low.

Next, he heard the men laughing about the fight. So he was beaten! At the thought, his rage flowed back in a red tide, and with it came fresh strength and oblivion to pain. He rolled over quietly and dropped to the deck. Pop sat on the side of his bunk, elbows on knees.

"Come on, soger," Joshua taunted. "I'm going to finish you off!"

"Huh?" Pop exclaimed, astonished. A man once beaten was supposed to stay beaten, and as for a boy, he should know his place without making such a nuisance of himself.

Joshua drove his fist at that badly bruised eye, but Pop raised his head in time to catch the blow on his nose. With a roar of rage he leaped up, and the fight was on again.

While Joshua had lain in his bunk, Pop's eye had swollen almost closed and his vision was impaired. So now he guarded it with his left fist held constantly against his cheek bone so that he could barely see over it and Joshua could no longer hit it at all. This left only his right hand for attack; and although Joshua could not hurt him, at least the boy was able to dodge that one fist without difficulty and even to land some stinging blows on the sailor's mouth. If Pop had been smart, he would have kept on in that fashion until the boy exhausted himself; but he was not smart and finally one blow on his mouth a little more painful than usual drove him to reckless rage again. His guard came down and his two fists started to swing. Instantly Joshua hit that eye. The mouselike swelling burst and a little blood trickled down into his eye, blinding him completely. He lowered his head and charged, fists flying like two windmills. Joshua threw himself to one side onto his hands, thrust out one foot, and tripped him. Pop lunged headlong into the bulkhead with a force that would have crushed an ordinary skull. He lay where he had fallen, face down.

The other sailors watched, expecting the boy to finish him off with his boots. But Pop was already finished, and in any case the brutal methods of the forecastle were repugnant to Joshua. To fight fiercely while one's enemy could fight back was one thing; to kick a man as he lay unconscious was a totally different thing. In Joshua's mind the fight was over. While he needed it, rage had given him strength; but now his rage was gone and he was exhausted. His knees sagged under him and he wondered if he could get into his bunk. He was dizzy with pain and exhaustion.

At that moment there came the telltale pounding on the hatch cover, and the voice of the mate, "La'board watch, turn out!"

As the sailors trooped past him, Joshua stood and felt his face. He decided he might not look too bad. His head ached cruelly, he had a puffy bruise, very tender, on his left cheekbone, and his lips were cut and swollen; but there was no soreness about his eyes.

A minute ago he had wondered if he could climb into his bunk; now he wondered if he could climb out of the forecastle. He might even be ordered aloft.

As the last man went up the ladder, Joshua took a dipper of water and poured it over his head. He looked down at Pop. There was no more anger in him and now they both had to face their common enemy. He poured a dipper of water over Pop's head. The man stirred, groaned, rolled over and sat up.

"La'b'd watch, Pop," he said. "That eye looks bad. Wash your face. Keep out of Mr. Wilson's way if you can."

Pop put one hand over his bruised eye and gently wiped

away the blood. He put the other on top of his head and groaned. Slowly he got to his feet. He sloshed water in his face, set his hat tenderly on his head, and went slowly up the ladder.

At his heels Joshua looked at that ladder. He set his hands on an upper rung and a foot on the bottom rung, and found that he could lift his weight. He went up. He stepped out onto the forecastle deck. The fresh, clean air helped to clear his head. Pop was already down on the main deck, his hat tilted over his eye. Joshua had not been missed and Mr. Wilson was walking aft, his back to the boy. There was some luck in the world, after all.

The crew was assembling aft, just below the break of the poop. The ship was standing smoothly down the Chesapeake, with no immediate need for any work to be done. Joshua joined the crew as fast as his wobbly knees would carry him.

The captain stood at the rail gazing down at his crew and, to Joshua's eye, looking insufferably cold and mean. He started speaking—something to the effect that if they were prompt and willing to carry out all his commands they'd find him an easy man to get along with but if they sogered, they'd find him a tartar. It was the usual talk at the start of a voyage. Joshua had heard it once before and now he paid no attention, but he was grateful for the rest. Thanks to the recuperative powers of a healthy young body, he was feeling stronger by the minute, but just the same, he was far from right, and he wished the captain would talk the watch away.

The captain talked for about five minutes; then the starboard watch was sent below and the larboard watch was ordered to set the staysails and studdingsails that the starboard watch had brought up from the sail locker and left on the deck.

Climbing the ratlines wasn't as bad as Joshua had expected. The shrouds sloped so steeply that he could lean forward, and he could climb with his arms as well as with his legs. The worst part was lifting his arms above his head, because of the bruises on his shoulder muscles. A good many of Pop's wild swings must have glanced off his arms and shoulders unnoticed at the time. With a speed that astonished him, he got out to the fore-topsail yardarm; and there he felt the world slipping away from him. He glanced down, but he couldn't see a thing. It was all black down there. It was black everywhere. . . .

Salt water stung his nostrils. He strangled. He struggled, wildly at first, then more intelligently. His face burst out into air. He coughed and strangled, but he got a breath. Then he heard that cry so terrifying at sea—"Man overboard!" and the horror of Amos's death swept over him before he realized that it was he himself who was overboard. He turned his head in the direction of the repeated cry. He was bobbing on the peaceful little waves of the sleepy summer Chesapeake, a short distance astern of the ship. He saw faces along the rail, heard commands, saw topsails backed, saw a bale of barrel staves rise between two men, poise fleetingly on the bulwark and topple overboard, and he swam to it. He was a poor swimmer, but he reached it. The ship was a cable length away, her topsails backed, her boat being lowered. The cool water was vastly refreshing. He rolled over onto his back on the bale of staves and lay flat, the warm sun beating down on him.

A fine sailor I am, he thought, shamefaced. Overboard on a day like this! I'll never hear the last of it. The ship as steady as a house. Pop, you won that fight, after all!

He was greatly rested, and as he climbed aboard the ship he thought he might be able to finish his watch after all.

When he came up over the bulwark and dropped, wet and streaming, to the deck, Mr. Wilson was waiting for him, fists on hips, black eyes flaming. Without a word he stood and looked Joshua over. He studied the telltale bruises on the boy's face. He ran his eyes insolently from the boy's head, slowly, down to his feet; then, just as slowly and insolently, from his feet back to his head. The scorn in his eyes made Joshua squirm inwardly but he refused to fidget. He held himself rigid, not moving a muscle, but he thought the mate would never speak. Almost anything would be better than that silent contemptuous raking from stem to stern.

When at last he did speak, it was in the same deceptively mild voice he had used that first day, just before he had blasted Joshua off the quarter-deck.

"A sea lawyer," he said, as if he were talking to himself. "Knows how to add and subtract. Should of stayed home with mama. Read a book about the sea, once, and now he calls himself a seaman. And I had to draw him for my watch!"

Joshua knew such mildness couldn't last, and he braced himself for the roar of rage that was sure to come. Behind Mr. Wilson he saw the entire crew—the starboard watch had poured out on deck at the cry of man overboard—and they were revelling in the show. Joshua's temper was rising, and anger renewed his strength.

Mr. Wilson changed his tone, but not to a roar. Instead

he spoke in a gentle voice of mock solicitude, like the purring of a huge cat. "Would it be too much, do you think, little lad, if I asked you to get up to the maintop for me? Or don't you feel equal to it?"

"I'd be glad to go to the main skysail yard for you, sir."

"If you would be so kind, then," said Mr. Wilson, still purring.

Joshua caught a main shroud as high above his head as he could reach, swung himself to the rail, and started slowly up the ratlines. That mainmast really was as tall as a modern ten or twelve story building, but to Joshua just then it seemed to stretch up and up into the mysterious blue dome of the sky and he was far from sure he could reach the skysail yard.

The futtock shrouds sloped outward at a sharp angle that turned Joshua's back to the deck and forced him to dangle entirely by the strength of hands and arms. He longed to go through the lubber's hole instead, but he went out and over the edge, hand over hand, and on up the main topgallant mast. His breath whistled between his teeth and it was a comfort to know that Mr. Wilson couldn't hear it. He kept right on going, slowly but steadily, until he reached the main skysail yard, and there he stood, one arm wrapped tightly around the mast, above him nothing but the polished brass ball that topped it. His lungs burned painfully. His mouth was full of cotton, and every muscle in his body quivered. As a very small boy he had learned to say his prayers at his mother's knee, and now he prayed unconsciously and fervently, "Dear God, don't let me faint again!"

He looked down to where Mr. Wilson and all the crew stood, their faces turned up to him. They appeared to be nothing but faces, and very small faces at that. He had no breath to spare for words but he waved his free hand and arm in a wide, triumphant gesture. Now came Mr. Wilson's voice, and in spite of the distance it was the full-throated bellow he had expected sooner. "Just stay right where you are 'til I call you! And if you want to take a dive off of that yard, go right ahead and do it—but if you do, your own mama wouldn't recognize you!"

"Aye, aye, sir!" Joshua replied in the strongest voice his laboring lungs could muster. He grinned, well pleased. Now he'd have a rest—and what a joke that would be on Mr. Wilson!

His knees were wobbling dangerously. He could not possibly stand much longer. He wrapped both arms around the mast and lowered himself ever so carefully until he sat on the spar, legs dangling in space. And right there he did stay until he heard the mate command, "Go below the larboard watch!"

CHAPTER SEVEN

MR. WILSON WAS NOT A CRUEL MAN BUT HE HAD A STERN sense of duty to the ship, and his black eyes burned with a fanatical light. He held a conviction that it was wrong to haze a seaman merely to satisfy a personal grudge. He would not haze the boy, he honestly believed, merely because the captain had knocked their two heads together. But if a seaman showed a tendency to get above himself, then it was a good thing for discipline to work the conceit out of him. And he had no trouble at all in convincing himself that Joshua was bursting with conceit, and that a severe hazing was exactly what he needed. It was at the captain's command that Joshua spent two or three hours of his own time every day on the ship's paper work, but Mr. Wilson overlooked that fact entirely and laid full blame for it on the boy. So he convinced himself with the greatest ease that it was his duty to haze Joshua, and he went at that duty with a zeal that was in proportion to his resentment of the captain's conduct toward him.

Because of Joshua's tumble overboard, it was evidently necessary to accustom him to work aloft. His first watch had been spent doing nothing aloft—in Mr. Wilson's opinion, a very scientific approach to the problem. Well, he could be hazed aloft. In fact, he could be worked pretty nearly to death aloft, and Mr. Wilson was just the man to do it.

When Joshua started each watch thereafter, the mate generally ordered him first to the main skysail yard, and from there, he kept the boy travelling back and forth, hand over hand, along the stays that connected the masts. Most of these trips were clearly useless, and were meant only to punish him by sheer hard work. There was a limit, though, to the amount of such climbing that the strongest sailor could do, and even the most fanatical mate dared not drive a man too hard, for fear muscles quivering from exhaustion would falter and let him fall to the deck.

There were exceptions to this routine, however. On alternate mornings, when the mate's watch swabbed the deck at sunrise, Joshua was on his hands and knees along with the other men. All the dirtiest, most disagreeable jobs were flung at him; but when these jobs were done, aloft he went. All the other sailors spent at least a part of their time at the braces or at other jobs on deck. They worked together, and there was companionship in their work. When they did go aloft, they did what had to be done, then slid down the stays to the deck again. By contrast, Joshua was required to spend nearly all his time aloft. He liked people. He was intensely friendly and sociable, and the worst feature of his hazing—though it is doubtful that Mr. Wilson understood that—was that he lived in a peculiar sort of solitary confinement a large part of his time. He worked alone at winding chafing gear on all the loftiest points in all that new rigging. It was work that could be sandwiched in between periods of climbing, in what might be called rest periods. And when all the chafing gear was done, he was set to tarring down all the standing rigging. He wasn't allowed to spend more than one watch a day on that, either, lest it be finished too soon.

This was a dull life for an active mind, but when Joshua got too bored, he could think of the drudgery of the countinghouse from which he had so happily escaped, and of the boys he had left behind to grow up pasty-faced and hump-shouldered over musty old ledgers, while his own hard-driven muscles were growing so fast he sometimes fancied he could see a difference from one Sunday to the next.

May passed and June came in, and still the weather held fine. And still the mate implacably hazed the boy, with no sign of relenting. Nearly every day in such weather a few of the sailors worked at unlaying old rope to make seizings, chafing gear and the like. When the little windlass was spinning, three men worked together, one to turn, one to feed and one to take off the yarn the other two untwisted and roll it into balls to be used as needed. It was easy, pleasant, sociable work. Joshua could hear the men talking and laughing together, and even the windlass had a jolly, chuckling sound—but he never got a hand on it. In this fashion days ran into weeks and the weeks into a couple of months. The *Sidney* sailed into the harbor of Cadiz, delivered her cargo, shipped another, and turned homeward; and still Mr. Wilson's hazing continued unabated.

Luckily the second mate had none of Mr. Wilson's disposition, for if he had added his own brand of hazing to the mate's he could have made the boy's life truly unbearable. As a rule the second mate considers it good policy to curry favor by hazing any man who is in hot water with either of his superior officers, but Mr. Grogan did not conform to that rule.

The position of a second mate, and his standing with the crew, bore little resemblance to that of the mate. The latter never went aloft, or put his hand to any dirty work. He took his meals with the captain and held himself aloof from the crew. A second mate ate alone, making his meals on the cold leavings of the captain and the mate. He had to work aloft with the crew and to put his hand to all the tar and slush and other dirty work they had to do. He rubbed elbows with them in the most intimate fashion, yet he had to keep their respect and maintain discipline; and there was only one way in which he could do it—by brutal beatings for any man who showed a disposition toward insubordination. Since captains were recruited from the ranks of mates; and mates, from the rank of second mate; few men were able to climb to that lofty eminence except by the hard and brutal road of many beatings. Mr. Grogan's ability to thrash any man on board was so evident that he seldom had to resort to such methods. The result was that under him, work generally went smoothly and happily.

Joshua not only liked him; he admired him immensely. He admired the speed with which he could lift his bulk about aloft. He was a monkey in the rigging; not a man on board could keep pace with him. He admired his height and his wide and massive shoulders. It was exactly the physique that Joshua fondly expected to have. And in fact, he had some reason to expect it, for his shoulders and chest were broad and deep, and strength was flowing into his fast-growing muscles in a rich red tide. But he was not gaining much in height.

The first reservation in his ardent admiration came when he heard Mr. Grogan say, " 'Tis meself that's twenty-five years old this day, and exactly half me life have I spent at sea."

When I am twenty-three years old, Joshua told himself, I'll say the same, and I won't be just a second mate, either.

Then one day he asked Mr. Grogan a question. It was one that he'd had in his mind from the start of the voyage, and it was the sort that Captain Chilton would have answered with pleasure, but he had never asked Captain Drysdale anything and evidently could not ask Mr. Wilson. Even Mr. Grogan, agreeable as he usually was, had not seemed very approachable for questions, but the matter bothered Joshua, and finally he decided to try it.

"Wouldn't it be better, sir," he said, "if we had single blocks on some of these light sails? Couldn't we shift 'em faster?"

"Eh? What is it to ye, Barney?"

"Why, sir, it seems to me we are pulling twice as much line through our hands on some of these light sails as we need to. We could brace 'em around with a straight line, or with single blocks. It would make faster handling. And in some places we could do better by changing the purchase of the lines."

"And what is it to ye?"

"Why, sir, I want to understand. Besides, if she were rerigged. . . ."

"Purchase! Rerigged! May God have mercy on yer soul,

Barney, if ever I get the idea ye are tryin' to get above yerself! Do yer work from the ears down, an' leave thinkin' to yer betters!"

A very blank expression flitted across Mr. Grogan's face before he interrupted, though, and Joshua rightly decided that the second mate's bluster was designed to conceal his ignorance of the subject. To Joshua, the geometry of a ship's rigging was clear, because it was one of the subjects on which Captain Chilton had drilled him so thoroughly during his year on the Chesapeake; and now, for a second time, he was forced to revise his opinion of Mr. Grogan—this time pretty drastically.

"Barney report to the cap'n in his cabin." The *Sidney* was unloading at Whetstone Point, and it was the voice of Pop at the forecastle hatch.

Now what has that fish-hearted brother-in-law of mine cooked up for me this time? Joshua wondered as he climbed the ladder and went aft. "Nothing good, I'll lay to that," he assured himself.

"Barney," said Captain Drysdale as the former entered the spacious stateroom for the first time in all the while he had been aboard the *Sidney*, "you've been checking the navigation; can you do it alone? Shoot the sun?"

"Yes, sir," said Joshua, perceiving that something momentous was afoot and deciding to plunge. "Moon, too, sir. I am almost ready for lunar navigation. I've been working hard on it."

Captain Drysdale's eyebrows rose slightly, but "Call Mr. Grogan, if you please, Mr. Barney," was all he said. It was enough.

"*Mister* Barney!" Joshua repeated to himself in wonder as he left the cabin. *"If you please, Mister Barney!* Whe-e-e-w!"

Only an officer was ever addressed as "Mister," and Captain Drysdale would be the last man afloat to use the title lightly, or to say "please" to a seaman, though it was the usual courtesy from captain to officer.

Mr. Barney found Mr. Grogan on the main deck. "The captain wants you in his cabin, sir," he said.

"What's up, Barney?" Mr. Grogan said. "You look pop-eyed."

Joshua grinned. "Search me, sir. Something's in the wind, but I can't guess what it is."

Mr. Grogan went aft, Joshua at his heels. Inside the captain's stateroom they stood, backs to the bulkhead, not venturing to be seated in any of the comfortable chairs screwed to the deck unless the captain invited them to do so; and the captain did not invite them. "Mr. Grogan," he said, his pale eyes intent on his second mate's face, "Mr. Wilson will not be sailing with us again." He paused, and the exciting speculations already scampering about in Joshua's mind began to take on clearer form.

"I can hire another mate," the captain said. "It would be the usual thing to do. But I like to see a young man better himself." He paused again, to let that sink in. Joshua, his dark eyes darting from one to the other, could find only blankness on Mr. Grogan's heavy features.

"Have you given any thought to your future, Mr. Grogan?"

"To—my future, sir?"

"That's what I said!"

"Why, sir," Mr. Grogan floundered, "I can't say as I

have." He added as an afterthought, "Not very much, that is to say, sir."

" 'Tis high time that you did. You don't want to remain a second mate all your life, do you?"

"Yes, sir. I mean, no sir."

"I could hire a new mate, but I like to see a young man better himself," the captain repeated. "Now if you would care to take the berth of mate, together with the privileges and most of the responsibilities that go with it, I'll make Mr. Barney my second mate, and have him do the navigating for you until such time as you can learn to do it yourself." The captain paused again. Mr. Grogan gulped.

"How does that strike you, Mr. Grogan?"

"Why, sir, I'd like that."

"Of course, until you are proficient in navigation, your wages will continue to be just what they have been. I couldn't pay you a full mate's wages until you can do full mate's work."

"Why, that's fair enough, sir. Thank you kindly for the chance, sir. I'll work hard to learn."

He's making me second mate, Joshua was thinking, and in fact, much more than second mate, and he isn't saying one single word to me! Just, "I'll have Mr. Barney do this, and do that." There was nothing unusual about that, though. It was strictly in character. Barney's apprenticeship was a binding contract, at a fixed wage, for seven years; and it began to be evident that long before the seven years had run out, he might be a full mate, with all of a mate's responsibilities, at the wage of an apprentice.

As he followed Mr. Grogan back to the main deck, he gave a moment's thought to the arrangement from the new mate's point of view. Presumably, under such an arrangement, the captain should spend some time coaching a man, as that should not be left to an inferior in rank; but Joshua was very suspicious. When Old Fish Eye claimed an altruistic motive for anything, it was high time to be suspicious. However, that was Mr. Grogan's lookout. Joshua couldn't see that he himself had anything to lose. Until Mr. Grogan could learn to navigate—but what then? Must I start, he thought, to play navigator, only to give it over to him as soon as he learns? *Suppose I learn lunar navigation before he learns solar navigation —once Old Fish Eye learns how much more accurate lunar navigation is, he'll never go back to dead reckoning and solar observations.*

The answer was so obvious it was startling.

On deck the new mate turned to his junior. "So 'tis *Mister* Barney now," he said with heavy emphasis on the "Mister." "Lad, ye're climbin' fast!"

"Right on your heels!" Joshua laughed.

"Will ye be so kind as to see about some books for me, Mr. Barney?"

"With pleasure, Mr. Grogan."

CHAPTER EIGHT

ELEVEN MONTHS PASSED, AND ON A SUNNY DAY IN JULY BARney was working aloft with the starboard watch. At the moment there was really very little for him to do. To keep his watch busy he had them winding on some chafing gear that could just as well have waited for the wear and tear of another gale. He took great pride in keeping the ship in apple-pie order; and he still enjoyed working aloft. He was one of the best navigators afloat, but he was still a boy in years and an incurable romantic at heart, and he had an undying love for the immensity of the cloud-dappled blue dome that arched so far above him. Around him—at a distance he could compute accurately for any elevation above the deck—lay the upbroken rim of the dreaming summer sea, forever alluring, forever remote and unattainable. The massive spars, the taut lines humming softly in the breeze, the straining canvas, the sweating sailors, his own iron-hard, bulging muscles—all made up a small world that was the exact, ever-advancing center of that vast, ever-advancing circle. Sometimes it disappeared in the fury of a storm, and always it was broken by the sight of land; but at sea it was always there and on such days as this it was measured by his own elevation above the earth's curve.

Hand under hand he dropped down a stay to the mizzentop, and from there he looked down upon his two superiors on the poop deck, the captain pacing slowly back and forth on the weather side, the mate standing moodily against the taffrail.

The captain's crafty bargain was working out better for Barney than he had dared to hope; but for Mr. Grogan it had turned out worse than he had foreseen. "Mate!" The combination apprentice-second-mate-navigator uttered the word under his breath and snorted in derision. His mind ran back to that day in August when Captain Drysdale had driven his miserly bargain. For a while after that, as the *Sidney* had lain at Whetstone Point, Mr. Grogan, in the pride of his new rank, had shown a tendency to strut the deck. But not for long. Oh, not for long! Scarcely had they dropped the Virginia capes astern on their next voyage than he had come upon the poop deck with a black scowl on his face. For several days, then, he had been in a foul temper. Everybody from the second mate on down had suffered for it. Joshua could take that trifling unpleasantness in unruffled calm, for it was nothing compared to what he had endured under Mr. Wilson; but not many days had passed before he had perceived that all was not well between the mate and the captain— and a duller man than Barney would have appreciated the threat to his own uncertain, unconventional rank.

For a week he had watched and waited; then he had decided to risk a hand in the business. "Captain helping you with your studies of navigation, Mr. Grogan?" he had asked, certain beforehand what the answer would be.

"Hah!" Mr. Grogan had snorted, glaring ferociously at his junior.

"You can't just figure it out from the books, you know. You've got to have help."

"Or another ship!"

"That's what I'm afraid of. But then you'd be just a second mate again."

"What's wrong with that?" Mr. Grogan had demanded truculently.

"Not a thing—only you did say you'd like to be mate, and in line for a command. Would you let me help you, sir? After all, I had mighty good help."

"You!" Mr. Grogan had glared. "You help me! Undermine yourself! Likely! Go soak yer head, Mr. Barney!"

"Where'll I be if you do quit? Don't you see, sir, I'll be better off if you stay on than if you quit and he hires another mate? I'll make a bargain with you. I'll help you all I can. When you get your ticket, you get a berth on another ship."

"What'll that get you? He'll still have to hire another mate."

"Mayhap. Mayhap not. By that time I'll be using lunar distances and I'll save him money over a new mate."

Mr. Grogan's slow wits had turned that thought about for a moment, his scowl slowly clearing. " 'Tis the sharp one ye are, Mr. Barney," he had said at last, "and mayhap ye are right. 'Twould be no stranger'n what he's done already for a little gain. Blessed if I don't take ye up on it."

That had been in August, and now it was another July. For almost a year Joshua had worked conscientiously at his part of the bargain, but he had not been able to do as much for Mr. Grogan as he had expected. The mate had no head for mathematics, and no education to fall back upon. Barney was perpetually amazed that anybody could be so stupid in matters that, to him, seemed so crystal clear. If they had been able to sit down together for an hour or so every day, it would have been different, but both officers could not leave the deck at the same time. No doubt Mr. Grogan had some lesson papers in his pocket right now, just waiting for the opportunity to hand them to his junior.

Eight bells rang. Hand under hand, Barney dropped swiftly down a stay. "Go below the starboard watch!" he commanded. He had work to do on the log, and he knew from the way Mr. Grogan eyed the captain that he did have some lesson papers and would not hand them over as long as Old Fish Eye remained in sight. Joshua had scarcely a minute to call his own, and he was impatient to get at the log. A second mate does not leave the deck merely because his watch has gone below, for he has many duties with the larboard watch as well. He is, in fact—or was in Barney's day—the busiest, hardest-working man aboard, for he spent a certain amount of time with every larboard watch. The crew called him "the sailors' waiter" because he had charge of the boatswain's locker in which were stowed the tools and materials such as serving boards, marlinespikes and all the other tools the sailors used, and these he had to dole out and keep track of, besides doling out such materials as marline and spun yarn and pitch.

In addition to all of this, Joshua had his work on navigation and the log, and on top of that he had to make up and correct lesson papers for Mr. Grogan, so the wonder was that he ever found time for sleep.

Captain Drysdale went below. Mr. Grogan walked down to the waist of the ship, where he met Barney, and a small bundle of papers changed hands. Joshua slipped it into his pocket and walked aft. When he had computed the position for the day, and had posted the log, he went on to his own tiny cubby, where he sat on the edge of his narrow bunk and hauled forth the papers Mr. Grogan had given him. They were covered with figures—problems in arithmetic set down in his own neat, orderly hand, and solutions in Mr. Grogan's unformed, gargantuan scrawl. Barney shook his head in despair. Imagine a log written up in that fist! It was a wonder to him that Mr. Grogan didn't quit the ship, for his progress was so slight that it seemed impossible he could ever qualify as a navigator.

Mr. Grogan did not quit, however. A second year rolled by, and half of the third, and the strange arrangement held firm, while the savings therefrom continued to pour into the captain's pocket.

It was December 22, in the year 1774, when Joshua was fifteen and a half years of age, that the *Sidney* sailed from Baltimore with a cargo of wheat consigned to merchants in Nice.

On the third morning after dropping the Virginia capes astern, the crew started, as usual, to pump ship. It was a task which, of late, had required about an hour every morning. Barney had felt some slight uneasiness over the increasing leakage at the start of so long a voyage; but that was a responsibility shared by Mr. Grogan and the captain; and the captain had not come near the ship while she was loading. On this morning, though, when the four men took hold of the handles of the big chain pump, they could not turn it at all. Barney called the carpenter. "Open the pump-well hatch, Chips," he ordered. "See what's wrong."

The carpenter peered into the pump well. There was concern on his face when he turned to Barney. "Well be stove, sir," he said. "Pipe broke and pump jammed."

Joshua looked into the well. The stoppage showed clearly. Planks along one side had broken under the weight of the cargo, the square plank pipe that should have run straight and true down the side of the well was broken, and sacks of wheat had forced themselves part way into the well, jamming the pump.

"Call Mr. Grogan," Barney said.

When the mate appeared and heard the report, he went immediately into the well. In a few minutes he was on deck again, his scowling face corroborating the carpenter's report.

"Can we repair it at sea?" Barney asked him.

"Not likely. Cargo's stowed too snug. I know, for 'tis meself that stowed it."

"You better go ahead and tell the captain, then. This course won't take us back to Norfolk."

It was no way for a second mate to speak to the mate, but Mr. Grogan turned without another word or show of resentment and went off slowly to Captain Drysdale's cabin. Barney watched him, noticed the droop of the broad shoulders, and sympathy was mixed with his own anxiety. What would the captain do now? It was a disturbing question from Joshua's point of view, but still he felt sorry for the half-baked mate who had to face the captain's wrath.

"Mr. Grogan!" Captain Drysdale exploded when the

mate had explained the situation, "are you responsible for the lading of this ship, or not?"

"I am, sir."

"Then do you mean to stand there and tell me there is any part of her that is too rotten for service, and you laded her in that condition?"

"That plankin' looked sound enough to me, sir."

" 'Looked sound enough! Looked sound enough'!" the captain mimicked him, his voice bitter with sarcasm. "Mr. Grogan, if I find that you are to blame for this, I'll break you for it. I am going into that well to see just how big a fool you may be!"

The captain hated to soil his clothes, but down the ladder in the pump well he went, and when he came on deck again he plunged into the hold, fuming and swearing, to make sure there was no possibility of shifting the cargo and making the repairs at sea. He was soon on deck again, and in a voice that cracked with rage he ordered the ship put about. "Dry rot!" he stormed. "Chief mate, and don't know dry rot when he sees it!"

Men were stationed below, in the forepeak and afterrun, while others on deck lowered buckets on ropes, and in that clumsy fashion they bailed her day and night for the three days' run back to Norfolk.

Six days' sailing time lost! Probably another week in port for repairs—two weeks wages and rations thrown away! Wharfage for unloading cargo! All to come out of the profits of the voyage! The captain was in a frenzy. He paced the quarter-deck, frequently striking his right fist savagely into the palm of his left hand. Joshua had never seen him in such a state. And during the three days it took to return to Norfolk, he was more glad than ever that he did not take his meals with his captain. He wondered that Mr. Grogan could eat anything.

When enough of the cargo had been removed for carpenters to get at the trouble, repairs were simply and easily made, but Captain Drysdale continued to vent his unabated wrath on that stubborn red head. Mr. Grogan endured it until the very hour the ship was to put to sea again, and then, as if he had deliberately waited until the moment came in which he could cause the captain the greatest inconvenience, he released the long-overdue explosion of his own temper, and with all the rich and racy eloquence to which he could lay his Irish tongue, and in a voice to be heard clear up into the town, he cursed his captain. And when he had finished, he turned on his heel and stalked off the pier.

Barney listened with a straight face and unbounded delight, for Mr. Grogan was saying so many things he himself had so long wanted to say. Now his satisfactory arrangement was wrecked, but he wasn't too worried because there was just the possibility that the penny-pinching captain would sign on a new second mate and promote the apprentice rather than sign on another mate; and it was worth something to hear the captain so eloquently told off.

Raging blood stained Captain Drysdale's face almost purple, and the veins on his neck and face stood out like whipcords. Barney watched him a little anxiously, fearing a stroke as he stamped up the gangplank yelling hoarsely at the first sailors he saw. "Noah! Pop! Get into the mate's cabin! Heave everything overboard! Everything! Bear a hand!"

The sailors dived down the companionway but in so

short a time that Joshua doubted they had gone beyond the foot of the ladder, they were on deck again, and evidently struggling to suppress broad grins. There was nothing there, they reported. He had cleaned it out.

The hypocrites! Joshua thought with delight. Mr. Grogan must have had their help, but even so, it was a wonder how he had got all his things out so quietly. Without a doubt every man in the crew had known in advance exactly what he planned to do. Certainly they had all been close at hand for the explosion when it came.

Captain Drysdale didn't hesitate. "Mr. Barney!" he roared. "Get sail on her. We've wasted too much time here! Get sail on her!"

"Aye, aye, sir," Barney replied calmly enough. He turned and gave his orders. Was the captain crazy? Joshua wondered but didn't care. The crew swarmed up the gangplank, up the ratlines, out upon the spars. Joshua's attention was absorbed in his work as the ship eased away from the pier, as sails broke out overhead, as sheets and braces were drawn taut. Now the captain would have to stand watch-and-watch with his apprentice until he could sign on another officer some four, perhaps five thousand miles across the sea, and by that time, without any doubt, the old skinflint would sign on a second mate for the sake of economy, and the apprentice would be a full-fledged mate in all but salary.

Had any ship, ever before, set out on a five-thousand-mile voyage officered only by a captain and a very youthful apprentice? Joshua doubted it very much, and dismissed the question.

Before he went to sleep that night, though, a thought that had come to him before the pump jammed, came forth again from those shadowy regions beyond the borders of consciousness. It peeped cautiously about, like a mouse peering from its hole in the baseboard to see if the cat has left the room. Was leakage increasing? An hour a day at the pump was not excessive—provided it remained an hour a day; but on the last voyage it had not required so long. And Gibraltar, the first port of call, was four thousand miles away, while their destination was almost a thousand miles beyond Gibraltar. However, the captain had never been receptive to suggestions from his apprentice, and Barney had discreetly held his counsel.

On the third morning out of Norfolk Captain Drysdale failed to appear on the quarter-deck at his usual hour. At breakfast time he still had not appeared. Barney's watch ran out but until the captain should relieve him, he could not go off duty. Finally he sent the cook for him. Doc reported that the captain was ill, and Joshua went at once to see him. He found the captain on his side, his legs drawn up, his face twisted in pain.

"I've got a pain in my guts, Mr. Barney," he gasped. He paused, panting. "Look after things today. Come to me if you are in doubt."

"Aye, aye, sir," said Barney. In spite of the intensity with which he despised him, he felt a great sympathy to see him suffer so acutely.

Toward nightfall Barney went again to see the captain, and was shocked at the change in him. The cabin was cold, but his face was beaded with sweat, his eyes were bloodshot, he looked haggard, and he writhed a little in his agony.

"I'm in a bad way, boy," he said, for the first time in three years calling Joshua by a friendly name. He paused, panting. "I've tried to make a man of you. I hope you'll bear that in mind, now I need your help."

"I didn't need you to make a man of me, sir," Joshua replied, astonished. "God Almighty did that. But I'll do my duty by you. Can I do anything for you now?"

"Drops!" he gasped, pointing to a large bottle of brown fluid that rattled about in the rack above his wash bowl. Joshua handed it to him, and he took a long pull on it and returned it. Joshua looked at the label. It read "Maredant's Antiscorbutic Drops." He sniffed; a powerful and revolting odor assailed his nostrils.

Barney paced the quarter-deck until midnight, then sent a man to his stateroom for a blanket. The weather was raw, with scudding clouds through which a half moon broke occasionally. The wind was blowing half a gale, the ship was plunging through the seas and sending fans of white spray leaping above her weather bow and blowing down her deck, with an occasional dollop of solid green water sloshing down off her forecastle. But the poop deck was dry enough.

"Call me if there is any change in the weather, Joe," Barney told the helmsman. He wrapped the blanket around himself and lay down against the lee fife rail.

The next day the captain was plainly worse. He called repeatedly for water but vomited most of it right back. Rum, Maredant's Antiscorbutic Drops and other concoctions from the ship's medicine chest came up even more promptly. Barney held a long conference with the cook, who by ancient custom of the sea was always doctor to the crew.

"I done tried most everything in the medicine chest, sir," he said. "Trouble is, cap'n, he pukes everything up so fast, can't nothin' stay down long enough to do no good. He sets pow'ful store by that there Maredant's Drops an' it shore is pow'ful stuff. You can jist feel it take aholt in yore guts. But he don't git no good from it if he don't keep it on his stummick, an' he don't keep nothin' on his stummick, seems like."

There was no more sweat in him. His skin was hot and dry, and he writhed and gasped with the pain. The sight of his agony stabbed Joshua, but there was nothing he could do and the immemorial law of the sea demanded his presence on deck almost continually. The ship and her entire crew, including the sick captain, were suddenly his responsibility and his alone.

On his next visit to the captain he said, "I will have to appoint a man from the crew to stand watch-and-watch with me, sir. Who do you suggest?"

The captain glared. "Suggest! *I* suggest to my *apprentice?*" But he writhed and gasped, and Joshua saw that he was dismissed. He returned to the deck and piped all hands. As they assembled on the main deck he stood at the rail looking down on them, studying their upturned faces, wondering if they knew—or would care—that their tight-fisted captain was in a desperate condition.

"Lads," he said, "Captain Drysdale is in a bad way. I need a man to stand watch-and-watch with me. Until the captain recovers, he will be my second mate. I appoint Matthew Barnes. Step forward, Mister Barnes."

Mr. Barnes blushed a brick red under his tan, but he stepped forward smartly.

"Mr. Barnes, you are in command of the starboard watch. Remember, lads, he is *Mister* Barnes. You will obey him exactly as you do me."

The crew accepted the appointment gravely. Barney looked them over carefully, from Pop, whom he had fought to a finish nearly three years earlier, to Dan Wilson, signed on at the start of this voyage. There were no grins of derision, no sly shifting of eyes. His appointment was accepted as a matter of course, and he was well pleased.

The captain's symptoms seemed contradictory, for while the pain abated after the second day, the fever and the nausea increased. He could not retain even a sip of water; his skin was on fire; his wits seemed dull and as time passed, they became more dull. He ceased to recognize either Doc, who was in attendance much of the time, or Barney, who went in to see him often. Gradually he sank into a coma.

When Joshua turned in on the fifth night a thought that would no longer be denied came and hammered insistently at his mind. If the captain died, Barney would no longer be an apprentice. Peggy loved the fellow, though, he reminded himself as he tried valiantly to put the thought from his mind.

CHAPTER NINE

IN THE MORNING JUST ONE WEEK AFTER THE CAPTAIN HAD been taken ill the cook came on deck looking very solemn. "Cap'n's dead, sir," he said.

"I thought likely he would be. Call Sam and get him sewed up. See that he gets a good sinker for his feet, and have a good job done on the sewing."

"Aye, aye, sir."

The *Sidney* had dropped the Virginia capes a thousand miles astern, but Gibraltar still lay three thousand miles away, and Nice was almost a thousand miles beyond Gibraltar. To complete the voyage would require ten thousand miles of sailing, the delivery of one cargo and the purchase of another. Several months would be required, and leakage was increasing. A prudent lad, in Barney's place, would put back to Baltimore. Mr. Smith would say he had done well. He might even make him second mate, but hardly a first mate. Not at the age of fifteen and a half years. On the other hand, if he completed the voyage and turned in a good profit, the old man could hardly refuse to make him a captain. Or so he reasoned.

To put the matter in that light was to answer it, as far as Barney was concerned, but the decision was not entirely his to make. The crew might refuse to follow so youthful a commander. He was in a sweat to put it to them, but the decencies must be observed.

The cook, bent almost double, backed up the steep companionway from the cabin to the poop deck with one end of the captain's rigid canvas cocoon in his hands. The sailmaker followed, bearing the other end. They laid it on a wide board. The topsails were backed, and with the wind roaring and banging in her mountains of canvas, all hands were piped to the lee rail amidships. Now the ship was caught motionless and the great seas rushed at her as if to make the most of an opportunity they knew would not last long. Spray blew across her deck and spattered the men as they stood about the bier, their tarred canvas hats in their hands.

Holding the book with fingers that trembled in spite of himself, Joshua read the solemn burial service, while the biting wind ruffled the untarred hair about his temples and strange little chills played along his spine. His voice did not sound quite right to him and he hoped the crew would not guess his true feelings but would impute his quavers to reverence. The end of the plank was raised, and the shrouded figure slid off and dived with a small splash into the sea.

Peg was really lucky to be rid of the fellow, he thought; and he added, So am I. There was a small chill in the pit of his stomach because of his desire to make the most of this opportunity and the fear that the men would not have enough confidence in him. They had taken orders from him readily enough as long as there was a captain to make the important decisions. Would they trust him now for such major decisions?

They were there all about him now. He could put the question to them where he stood, but he did not believe he could speak to them without betraying his anxiety. To gain time, he made for the companion ladder to the poop deck. His knees lifted his weight only with the greatest difficulty. He tried to moisten his lips with his tongue, but the saliva in his mouth had turned to cotton. He stood at the rail and watched the men assemble at his feet, and shame flooded him that he should fail himself at so critical a moment.

To his impatience they seemed to move with deliberate reluctance; and yet the moment when he must speak was upon him much to soon.

Well, there they stood, waiting, all eyes turned up to him. He had to speak. His knees felt queasy and so did the pit of his stomach, but he was agreeably surprised to hear how clear and strong and natural his voice rose above the roar of the wind and the banging of the sails and the sounds of the seas against the ship.

"Lads," he said, "I have got to make a decision. I do not believe I have the right to command you to continue this voyage. If you decide among yourselves that you are afraid to continue with me, we will put back to Baltimore and ship another captain, and a mate. You know me, but you don't know what sort of captain you will get. We have been at sea ten days. It may take us six more weeks to reach Nice, or even Gibraltar. In my opinion, if you have confidence in me, it is your duty to proceed. What do you say? Will you go with me?"

The men shuffled their feet and glanced furtively at one another, and Barney knew a moment of black despair.

"Well," he said bitterly, "out with it. What do you say? Pop, what do you say?"

"Will she float, sir?"

"Aye," said red-headed Pat Moran. "Will she stay afloat long enough? Her seams opens up so bad on de wedder side ye could fling a rat trew 'em, sir!"

"If that's all that's bothering you, life is just as sweet to me as it is to you, and I'll trust the old girl if you will. Is that all that's bothering you? All of you?"

"Aye, aye, sir," came as a confused murmur from all hands, with much nodding of heads.

"Good lads," Barney said. "Then do I understand you want to go ahead with me?"

The *ayes* were repeated, with more nodding of heads.

"Then that is settled," said Barney. His chest filled with a deep breath as if a tight band were released from it. His eyes ran once more over the faces of the men who had so willingly ratified his right to supreme command. They ran forward over the splendid ship, and up in to her vast cloud of canvas. His ship! His ship! The thought sang in his soul, but he brought his eyes back to his crew, and his thoughts to the business in hand.

"The next thing," he said, "I will have to make Mr. Barnes my mate, and I will appoint Joseph Thompson second mate. Mr. Thompson, step out! Lads, remember, he is Mister Thompson, and you will obey him exactly as you do me."

The crew settled down smoothly under their new officers, but as the days passed the leaking increased rather rapidly, and the hours of pumping increased accordingly. This was a nuisance, for the crew was already shorthanded, having lost two hands when Barnes and Thompson became officers.

The *Sidney* was a new ship, and such leakage was a puzzle to Barney, for it seemed out of all reason. Pat Moran had said that the weather seams "opens up so bad ye could fling a rat trew 'em," and there was some basis for that picturesque exaggeration. In a sailing ship the pressure of the wind on the sails is transmitted down the shrouds to the hull, and sooner or later the strain causes the seams to gape a little on whichever side happens to be the weather side at the moment. The most obvious explanation for the *Sidney*'s leaking seemed to be her unusually tall masts, with their great leverage, and this explanation immediately suggested dousing her skysails. Barney was inordinately proud of those skysails, and he was reluctant to blame them, but now he furled them, determined that if the leakage decreased noticeably he would send down skysails and skysail masts. Leakage continued unabated, however, and since his problem seemed to be to make port before it got completely out of hand, he spread them once more to the breeze.

The time came when one hour in every two had to be spent in pumping, and the men were turning anxious eyes on Barney and murmuring among themselves. And still the leakage increased. There was little sleep for anybody, for when men weren't on watch they spent part of their time at the pump, and exhaustion began to show on all faces. Even Mr. Barnes and Mr. Thompson took their turns at the pump, and Barney spent long hours at the wheel.

On a course to Gibraltar the *Sidney* was a thousand

miles south of the route to England, and the weather was mild and pleasant for January and February. Some days the sky was heaped with cloud formations that Joshua always called "God's washing hung out to dry," while on other days not a cloud could be seen in all the vast blue dome and the ship moved over a sea as trackless as the space between the stars. To their south lay the Sargasso Sea, which all sailors dreaded because of the vast beds of sea weed that were said to entrap vessels and hold them until their crews starved and their hulls rotted and sank; but Barney's crew was too weary and too busy to think much about Sargasso weed, or even to enjoy the delightful contrast with the North Atlantic winter voyages.

While he had been a second mate, Joshua had worked and had fraternized with the sailors, and the vastness of the sea had never seemed lonely; but a captain cannot fraternize much with anybody and the lofty eminence he had attained so suddenly seemed, to his friendly nature, as remote as the North Star. At the start of this same voyage he had led the sailors, monkeylike, through the rigging in obedience to commands that originated down on the quarter-deck, but now it was he who stood on the quarter-deck and originated the commands, while other men raced about aloft. Before, he had borne a goodly share of responsibility, but now he had it all, and it was magnified by that ominous increase in the leaking.

And as the leaking increased, one question hammered continually at his mind. It dogged him as he watched the stream of clear sea water that gushed from the big chain pump, but it was worst of all when it came between him and his sleep. Would he be able to keep the ship afloat?

While they were still two hundred miles from Gibraltar

the pump was turning twenty-four hours of every day with four men driving it, and the crew were taxed to the limit of their endurance. At least, so Barney thought; but he was about to learn what men can do when necessity drives them. A storm was brewing. Joshua didn't wait for it to strike but called weary men from their bunks and sent them aloft to take in sail. It was well that he did, for it came with incredible speed. It howled down out of the north and before his preparations were quite complete he was in the grip of a screaming gale.

Dear God, he thought, am I going to Davy Jones's locker? And almost within sight of port? Well, if I do, I might as well go with a bold face as a sheepish one!

He doubled the force on the pump, and the men lashed themselves to the handles lest boarding seas carry them away.

When the crew saw that their captain was determined neither to heave-to nor to run before the gale, they turned terrified faces upon him, but he ignored them and held stubbornly to his course. He did not know whether he could survive on that course, but he was certain that if he let the storm blow him far from it, he would founder before he could recover the lost ground.

For twenty-four hours the storm raged, and then it blew itself out.

Sullen faces and black looks greeted Barney on all sides. To a man, the crew held him responsible for their plight. He'd have to do something, and do it quickly, or they'd get completely out of hand. He was at the wheel when Mr. Barnes came up out of the cabin and went down to the main deck. Joshua decided to unbend a little before he lost everything. A captain couldn't offer excuses or plead his cause—but he could gloat a little, and he proceeded to do it. In a voice pitched to be heard the length of the ship he called, "We made it, Mr. Barnes! We made it!"

"Aye, sir. I never thought we would, sir!"

"You wanted to run before it, didn't you, Mr. Barnes?"

"Aye, sir."

"Know where we'd be now if we had?"

"A weary ways from here, sir, anyway."

"I'll tell you where we'd be. We'd be a hundred and thirty or forty miles south-west of here and bound straight for Davy Jones's locker as sure as the devil because leaking like she is, we'd never beat back against this wind. We made a hundred and twenty-five miles during the gale and we're right ker-slap-dab on our course, and only about seventy-five miles from the Strait of Gibraltar. We can dock her there, and calk her. The rate we're going now, we ought to be in dock and free of the pump in another ten or twelve hours."

"Aye, sir. 'Tis easy to see now you was right, but I couldn't see it before."

Barney left it there, hoping the knowledge would seep into the minds of the weary crew and restore him to their good graces, but watch them as he would, he could see no response to the good news.

The wind was abating, and Barney continued to make more sail as the ship could stand it. He was driving her at a furious pace. A heavy sea still ran. They shipped no more water over their bulwarks, but huge, gleaming white fans of spray burst over the port bow and the racing crests reached greedily for the lee rail.

Toward sunset Joshua ordered Mr. Barnes to see that

a very sharp lookout was kept from the masthead, as they should be within the Strait of Gibraltar by dawn if they could maintain their present pace, but if he was just a little out in his calculations they might easily pile up on the coast of Africa or Spain during the night.

At these words the men at the pump did raise their heads and look a little cheered.

The sky was cloudless and the moon rose early, so that a shore line could be seen at a safe distance. The wind fell off rapidly, though, and crack on sail as he would, Barney could not maintain his speed. He was on deck at dawn anyway, his eyes searching the sea ahead, and a few minutes before the sun's red disc peered above the horizon, down from the masthead floated that sweetest of all sounds to the sailor long at sea—"Land h-o-o-o!" Again and again the lookout cried the words for sheer delight, drawing them out and all but making a song of them, as if he could not bear to let go of them. And at this the crew did raise a feeble cheer.

Barney took his glass and raced aloft. To larboard he could see the mountains of Spain, blue in the distance. To starboard, Morocco. Just as he focused his glass on the strait that opened a point to the north of his course, the sun burst from the sea, and it was impossible for him to tell whether he had actually seen the Rock of Gibraltar or just a wisp of gray cloud. However, it didn't matter. He needed a good landfall and he had made a very good one. Fifty miles more and he'd dock his ship. He returned to the deck, took the wheel, and told the helmsman to get some sleep and then report for duty at the pump.

Fifty miles! Ten hours, at least! Could his crew keep her

afloat that much longer? But no! They wouldn't have to. Through the Strait of Gibraltar there ran a current that flowed eastward incessantly at a speed of six knots! Not a tidal current, reversing itself every few hours, but a constant, God-sent current that would add its speed to that of the ship. Oh, good current, kind current; good, kind, God-sent current!

He had still ten miles more to go before the shores of Spain and Africa would converge enough to give the current its best speed, before that current would take the *Sidney* lightly upon its mighty back and bear her and her crew on to port.

He began to count the minutes and to estimate his speed —ten minutes, one mile; forty-nine still to go. Twenty minutes, forty-eight miles still to go.

There were now always four men at the pump, and they were relieved every thirty minutes. Every three miles. Could four men be expected to carry the *Sidney* on their backs for three miles? It required six or eight pallbearers to carry a casket to the grave, and a casket contained only one corpse. Eight corpselike figures sprawled on the deck where they had collapsed when they had been relieved from the pump.

Five bells! Forty miles still to go. Mr. Barnes jerked the laniard on the clapper, and Mr. Thompson roused four of those corpselike figures and sent them to the pump. Barney watched them anxiously. They drove it. They drove it more briskly than the four they had relieved. Even one hour's sleep was a boon—when it came often enough. When there was no work aloft between tricks at the pump.

"Drive that pump, you lubbers! Drive it! Break those pump handles! Break that chain! Break your backs! Break any bloody thing, only drive it!"

Six bells! Five more miles through the water. Add a couple of miles at least for the current as it funnels from the wide Atlantic into that narrow strait. Only about thirty-eight miles still to go!

A light smoke streamed down to leeward from the galley fire.

"Give 'em a tot of rum when they are relieved, Mr. Thompson. See they rest a while before they eat."

Seven bells! Only about thirty miles still to go. The current was gaining speed as it crowded between the continents.

Eight bells! Only about twenty miles still to go. The *Sidney* was riding the center of the current, for there it would be swiftest. She was in the full grip of that good, kind, God-sent current, and to its speed she was adding her own. Ten or eleven knots she must be making; perhaps even twelve.

How strange the sky was, there dead ahead! The ship was travelling at a speed of ten or twelve knots to meet that sky, but the sky was rushing down even faster to meet the ship.

One bell! Only fifteen or sixteen miles still to go. Barely two points off the larboard bow loomed the mighty Rock. But what of that sky? And the breeze was falling off!

"All hands to take in sail! All hands! All hands!"

Barney set the ship upon the starboard tack and put the wheel in a becket. He sent the cook and the carpenter to keep the pump turning, however slowly, and he went to help his officers and his exhausted crew take in sail.

The breeze died dead away.

The sails came in, but slowly. Barney was aloft once more, driving his crew, driving himself, working like a man possessed. The weary crew was sluggish and rebellious. Why work themselves to death taking in sail in a flat calm? But still Barney drove them. He furled all sails but the topsails, and those he double-reefed. Now he was close-hauled, but for what? On what tack? There was not a breath stirring.

From shore to shore of the strait the water became churned as if by a gigantic, invisible harrow that advanced upon the ship with terrible speed. And then the gale struck.

Barney had never known a worse one. Right out of the Mediterranean it came; right through the strait; and it kicked the poor old crippled *Sidney* squarely in the teeth.

Well, the current would hold her up against it if the crew could keep her afloat, and now he was on the starboard tack and she'd sidle over a bit toward Spain and the Rock. But the Rock was still twelve or fifteen miles away.

Dear God, must You sink me only ten or twelve miles from safety? Must you sink me in plain sight of port?

Once again his officers and crew turned terrified faces to him. They felt certain they were doomed to swift destruction unless he would turn and run before the gale. They said so, and this time Barney did not drive them. Instead, he went down on the main deck and called them about him and he raised his voice above the shrieking of the gale, while the men huddled in the lee of the weather rail and water sloshed knee-deep in the lee scuppers.

"Lads," he shouted to men not ten feet from him, "if we turn tail now, we'll founder before we can beat back to where we are this minute! We can't give an inch! Listen to this! There is a current that runs strong and swift through this gut! It will take us in! All we have to do is to keep her afloat and ride the good current! I am no sky pilot, lads, and I know naught of such things, but if the Almighty had it in for us, would he send that good current to take us in? Just keep her afloat, lads. God Almighty will do the rest!"

The crew knew of that current but in their exhaustion had forgotten about it until Barney reminded them of it. The thought that God was with them put new life into them, for however irreligious they might be in port, at sea, and especially in a gale, they were profoundly convinced of His power and glad to have Him on their side. Men all but dead on their feet gained new strength from some reservoir deep within themselves, and they strove with a last frantic energy at the big pump, while Barney wrestled single-handed with the bucking wheel.

The Rock, and the shores of the strait, were blotted out by the rain, but Barney felt certain he was near the center of the current because of the choppy seas they drove through. The wind against the current tore its surface to tatters and flung geysers skyward, to crash upon the deck.

The carpenter came to the poop deck where Barney struggled with the wheel. "Water be gainin', sir."

"Blast the water!" Barney roared. "Let the well alone! Get below there, and help with the buckets!"

The seas leaped aboard the ship, crashed down upon her deck, and mauled the men lashed to the pump. The current still held her against the gale, though, and their sails, close-hauled, drove her gradually across the strait. The wind died down. The clouds thinned and blew away. The great rock loomed ahead.

The *Sidney* ran into calm water. No more seas crashed upon her deck, but the men were so numb with exhaustion they appeared not to know. The ship glided softly into the lee of the great rock. On the eddy of the dying gale, she slid softly into the harbor.

CHAPTER TEN

THE SHIP WAS AT ANCHOR, BUT THE WATER IN HER HOLD WAS
gaining on her pump. Before Barney could dock her and
count her safe from sinking, however, he had to secure
permission from the local office of the British Admiralty,
for Gibraltar was strictly a naval and army outpost. He
ordered his gig lowered and set out across the harbor for
the shipyard that he could see about a mile away.

"Sir," said one of his oarsmen, "it do look like mighty
little water be comin' off of her."

Barney glanced back over his shoulder. Truly, only
the barest trickle of water ran from her scuppers. Now
that they were in port, it seemed that the men on the
pump had collapsed, as a runner does when he has finished
his race and broken the tape. Barney altered his course
and drove his oarsmen for the nearest British frigate.
There, when he had been permitted to come aboard, he
explained his plight to her captain and requested two
relays of fresh men for his pump. The captain immediately
ordered an ensign to take eight men for Barney's chain
pump and four more for the portable pump that all warships carried, and which he added to the help Barney
had requested. The ensign and his twelve men and his

portable pump went off at a fast pace, and Barney, vastly
relieved, turned once more toward the Admiralty office.

Nightfall found Barney standing on his poop deck,
relaxed, free from immediate anxiety, and very grateful
for the strange, dead feeling of the deck under his feet.
The *Sidney's* keel rested on hard-packed sand, and he
might have stood on solid rock for all the motion he could
feel under him. He became conscious for the first time of
his own great weariness; and he went below and to bed.

The "dock" at Gibraltar was merely a shelving beach
on which a vessel, after being unloaded, could be run
aground and hove down. In that position one half of her
bottom could be brought out of the water to be worked
upon. Then she could be floated, turned, and hove down
upon her other side. So far, though, she had not been
unloaded, and she was deep in the water. She was aground
and could not sink, but water could rise in her and ruin
her cargo. Her pump, manned by the borrowed crew,
continued to labor while Barney slept. If it had once
ceased, he would have awakened immediately.

When he did wake, the sun was high and he saw that
he had slept for fourteen hours. He stretched luxuriously,
dressed carefully, and went ashore, where he petitioned
the vice-admiralty court for a survey of his ship. It was
granted, but before it could be carried out, the ship must
first be floated and warped over to a pier, and a large part
of her cargo removed. Barney watched this removal with
anxiety, and was relieved to see that very little of it had
been damaged.

The survey showed, however, that costly and time-
consuming repairs would be required. Some of the hull
planking was edged with rot, and calking had been washed

out by the sea. Some of the treenails—those long wooden pegs used instead of nails to fasten the planking to the frames—had rotted, and water had got deep into the frames, causing rot in them also. Joshua already knew something about ship design and construction and now he began to learn something about lumber. White oak resists decay better than red oak or black oak. Even among the white oaks, he learned, there is a difference. And of the lumber from any given tree, heartwood is much more resistant to decay than sapwood. Some of his hull planking had been edged with sapwood; and some of the treenails were so far gone there was no knowing what kind of wood they had been. The cost would run far beyond the amount of money carried aboard for the ordinary expenses of a voyage.

Barney sat in his spacious stateroom and read these details with dismay. Repairs that would cost well over six hundred pounds sterling! He looked at the deck timbers above his head, and at the hull timbers that framed the stern. They seemed massive enough to last forever. But planks in the pump well had rotted out before the start of the voyage, and as he digested the details of the surveyors' report it began to seem little more than a miracle that the hull had held together for the voyage. He thought of the terrific wracking it had survived during that gale in the Strait of Gibraltar. Why she hadn't come all apart and taken her captain and her crew to the bottom with her right there was such a marvel that he almost ceased to worry over what he would do, for thankfulness that he was still alive.

Still, something had to be done, and as he brought his mind back to that stern necessity he thought bitterly of the fact that he had got command of a great ship only to find that she was a wreck. Would he sell her here for her cargo, and take passage for home? Hardly. Yet this was a naval and military outpost, and most likely there was not a banker within a few hundred miles.

Still, something had to be done. That was a necessity he could not escape. He got out his best shore going suit, and was shocked to find how he had grown. True, the waistcoat had been a little tight when he had left Baltimore, but now it would not button at all until he expelled all air from his lungs and shrank his chest down like a clenched fist, and then, when he did inhale, three buttons flew across the room and bounced off the bulkhead. The coat was noticeably short in the sleeves and he had the uneasy feeling that if he took a normal breath it would split wide open between his shoulders. The sailmaker soon remedied the waistcoat by moving the buttons to the edge of the garment, but the coat would have to serve. No doubt there would be tailors on the Rock, even though there might be no bankers.

Scarcely breathing, he went on deck and ordered out his gig, and uncomfortably conscious of his exposed wrists, he was rowed smartly to the nearest British merchantman. Captain Johnston, her master, proved to be a ruddy, round-faced Briton with bright blue eyes; and his surprise, when Joshua introduced himself as master of the finest merchant ship in the port, was plain to see.

As Barney explained his situation, he forgot his too-tight coat and he told a story of the voyage that held the captain fascinated to its end.

"You ain't in too bad a place, though," he said at last. "You see Murray and Son. There ain't many business people in the town, for a fact, but the Murrays are as good as you'd find anywhere. They'll treat you right."

"Bankers?"

"Traders. Bold traders. Go in for anything good. Leastwise, Murray, Senior, is. Don't know much about the son. Just a young boy—twenty-five or so. Ain't settled down yet."

The next morning at sunrise Barney set his crew to work sending down his top hamper. The ship would have to be careened on the beach and her masts unstepped because her shrouds would all have to be ripped loose in order to replace her hull planking. When the job was well along and he thought late-rising landlubbers would have got down to their counting houses, he went into the town to call on the Murrays. He was met by a pleasant young man who, as Captain Johnston had said, appeared to be about twenty-five—sandy-haired, blue-eyed, sun-tanned. Taller than Joshua by half a head, with a good pair of shoulders and well-muscled calves.

"I am Mr. Murray, Junior," he said in reply to Joshua's inquiry. "Can you tell your business to me?"

"I could, but Captain Johnston said I would have to see you and your father together. He seemed to know you well and he spoke very highly of you."

That neat little speech opened the door to the inner office. Barney found Mr. Murray a genial-looking gentleman with iron-gray hair and steel-gray eyes, and a complexion even more ruddy than his son's. His face was smooth except for the fine wrinkles that radiated from the corners of his eyes. "A mighty keen man of business," Captain Johnston had called him, and he looked the part. Joshua liked him at once.

Mr. Murray greeted him cordially, leaned back in his comfortable, high-backed chair, set the tips of his fingers together and his elbows on the chair arms, and settled down to the discussion that seemed to be in the wind.

"Captain Barney of the *Sidney*," he repeated Jack's introduction. "You brought her in through that levanter a week ago. A daring thing to do."

"It was the only thing I could do. She'd have foundered otherwise. So you know about her?"

"I know about every ship that puts in here. I understand you have an extensive repair job to be done."

"Yes, sir. Expensive, too. That's what brings me to you. I have a valuable cargo of wheat for Nice and I can't go any further. I need a loan. Captain Johnston thought you might be interested in the business."

"What security did you have in mind, Captain?"

"A bond, secured by my cargo, and payable on delivery."

"A bottomry bond would be to your advantage. The consignee should pay, under the law."

"Could I hold him to that?"

"You can call on him before delivery and request acceptance. If he doesn't want to take it up, you can dispose of your wheat elsewhere."

"You mean, sir, that he would have to add the cost of the repairs to the price he has agreed to pay for the wheat?"

"If he accepts it. He doesn't have to accept it, but it is customary."

"That way, it wouldn't cost my owner a cent!"

For half an hour, then, the merchant questioned Barney on the ship, on his crew, and on his life ashore and afloat. He had come prepared for a searching inquiry. He produced the log, the report of the surveyors, and even his articles of apprenticeship. Mr. Murray studied them all carefully and asked an astonishing number of questions.

"Of course you realize," he said at last, "that since you are a minor I might be unable to enforce a contract if you sought to evade it, and any loan I might make would have to be based more on my faith in your integrity than on the nature of the security."

Barney knew a moment of sheer desperation such as no hazard at sea had invoked, for he had already come to like Mr. Murray and to feel that here was the man—if one could be found—with whom he could do business; and if Mr. Murray just couldn't trust him, what was there for him to combat? Or where could he turn? But it was for an instant only, for Mr. Murray turned to his son and asked, "What do you say, Jack? Shall we see Captain Barney through?" and Jack immediately replied, "Yes, sir! I'm in favor of it." And Joshua's spirit soared.

"Good," said Mr. Murray, and they drew up the papers and signed them and Barney set forth with a light heart to get the work under way. It would be a tedious job, running into weeks. Still, it was routine carpentry, and nothing to worry about.

First, she had to be beached again, but this time it was important to beach her as high on the sand as possible so the carpenters could work all the way down her exposed side to her keel, and that meant riding the spring tide up the beach. True, the tidal range in Gibraltar harbor is slight, being only 2.3 feet on the average and 3 feet on the spring tides that follow the full and new moons; but even that difference would be important to the carpenters. The next full moon would come on March 17th, and Barney drove his men hard to be finished by that date.

Up from the hold came the last of the grain. Out came the masts, and when the spring tide was at the flood the *Sidney*'s hull had been relieved of every ton of removable weight. With fore- and aft-lines to the beach she was drawn up until the full length of her keel rested upon the hard-packed sand. The tension in her lines canted her shoreward, and as the tide ebbed, she settled on her bilges. On the low tides the carpenters could walk around her.

In the morning as Captain Barney stood on the upturned side of the hull and watched the carpenters assemble below him on the sand, their sharp-edged tools in their hands, he felt a wholly unexpected and curious little pang of regret for the vanished beauty and grace and dignity of his ship. To him she was more than just a thing of grace and beauty. She was almost a living, breathing creature. Nothing could be further from its natural element than a great ship, stripped of masts, spars and rigging and spewed out upon the sand; nothing, to Barney, could seem more helpless. And now came these little men with their gleaming tools, to rip and tear his helpless giant. A silly whim, unworthy of a man, and he brushed it from his mind. The carpenter foreman was climbing the ladder from the sand to speak to him. Head, then shoulders, then torso, he rose above the rail—a sour-looking old party, his coppery hair and spade-shaped beard well streaked with gray.

"Mornin', Captain," he said in an offhand manner that fell far short of the respect due to the master of a great ship in that age of formal courtesy. His eyes did not meet

Joshua's but dwelt on the boy's beardless cheeks in a fashion that reminded him of his youth. When, at Captain Drysdale's death, he had moved into the captain's spacious stateroom and had found there the only mirror on board the ship, he had anxiously examined his cheeks for the first signs of a beard and had found none. The Murrays plainly held it to his credit that he could command a great ship before he could grow a beard; but this sour-looking old foreman managed to convey the feeling that a beardless boy did not merit the title of captain; and Barney immediately felt a rising antagonism.

"Good morning, Mr. McGregor," he said, and stopped there.

"Colonial-built?" said Mr. McGregor, with a disdainful thump of his heel on the planking under his feet.

"Clyde-side," Barney snapped.

That carried the battle right into the foreman's native Scotland, and the sneer with which he had said "colonial-built" was replaced by a flush of anger. His yellow-green eyes met Barney's for a moment and encountered a flame that turned them aside.

"And how many strakes will ye have removed at one time, Captain?"

It was a shrewd question, since he had every reason to expect that a beardless boy flung suddenly upon the quarter-deck would fall headlong into his trap, but then, he could not know of Captain Chilton's teaching. Joshua knew, though, that as the hull lay upon its bilges on the hard sand its dead weight would tend to warp it out of shape, and if many strakes, or hull planks, were ripped off at one time, the force of gravity would work its will upon the hull and a curve would come into the keel.

And he saw plainly that Mr. McGregor had deliberately set a trap for him; for no ship carpenter could fail to know so elementary a fact.

"You are the foreman on this job," Barney told him, "and it is for you to say how many strakes should be ripped off at one time. But if you rip off more than one at at a time I will know you don't know your business."

The old man had laid himself wide open to that retort, and a derisive snicker from the carpenters awaiting his orders at the foot of the ladder told him plainly that the conversation had been overheard.

"It will cost ye a pretty penny!" was the best answer he could lay his tongue to before he turned and scrambled back down the ladder.

Barney remained standing where Mr. McGregor had left him. Plainly he would have to watch that foreman.

In midmorning a messenger came to the ship with a note for Captain Barney. It was from Mr. Murray and proved to be an invitation to luncheon. Surprised and pleased, he sent his acceptance by the same messenger. Then he thought of the clothes he should wear, for everything he had was much too small for him. Oh, well, he could laugh that off. He and Mr. Murray and Jack had already laughed about it, and Jack had taken him to the tailor who made clothes for the Murrays and a new suit was promised for this very evening. That would be no help for luncheon, though, and he begrudged the time from the ship that would be required to go to the tavern and change. He might as well go as he was. Everything he had was equally small. His bulging thigh muscles threatened to burst his breeches and the increased width of his shoulders took up too much of the sleeve length of his coat, but the ruffles of his shirt cuffs would help to cover his wrists. He shrugged that matter off and called Mr. Barnes.

He had a much better crew than he could hope to recruit on the Rock if he let these men scatter, and he had determined to keep them together and to use them as much as possible on the unskilled labor of the repairs; for while they were not carpenters, there would be much fetching and carrying to be done. Now he told Mr. Barnes to keep a sharp eye on everything while he went off to lunch; and at noon he set out for the countinghouse.

His mind was free of the cares that had beset him on earlier trips through the town, and he noticed with lively interest the cosmopolitan nature of the crowds in the narrow, dirty, foul-smelling streets. Gibraltar was a crossroads of world trade, visited by ships from all the seven seas. Men of dozens of nationalities swarmed into and out of its shops, haggled over prices, lounged about, strolled, walked or hurried on their business; gabbled, laughed or quarrelled, according to their natures. Swarthy Spaniards rubbed elbows with their ancient enemies, the Moors. A Greek or two; Italians; a pair of Turks; Egyptians; Ethiopians; huge black men and smaller brown men from many nameless tribes deep in Africa; tall, fierce-looking men in turbans Joshua thought must have come all the way from India; two Chinamen, their pigtails down their backs; big, blond Scandinavians; the nondescript riffraff of British jails with which the Royal Navy had to fill out its crews; red-coated British soldiers from the garrison on the Rock; and the native Scorpions who were a blend of heaven alone knew how many races. And the babel of tongues that assailed his ears was as polygot as the types he saw.

Fifteen minutes of walking brought him to the countinghouse.

Jack greeted him cordially and told him that the captain of one of the British frigates was soon to join them.

Joshua was elated at being included in such august company. Masters of merchant ships liked to make sulphurous remarks about the toploftical airs assumed by the commanders of warships in general and the British ships in particular. Barney did not share the feeling; but then, he had not been subjected to the overbearing arrogance of a British naval captain. Captain Tisdale, to whom he had appealed for help from sinking when he first anchored at Gibraltar, had been a most gracious and delightful gentleman and Barney hoped that it would be Tisdale with whom he would be lunching today. In that, though, he was disappointed. Captain Wilder, when he entered the countinghouse a few minutes later, seemed a different breed altogether. He was tall, with the heavy, powerful shoulders that Barney admired and hoped to develop before he stopped growing. His long, horsy face with its stubborn jaw was as deeply tanned as any other veteran seaman's, and his bearing was assured to the point of arrogance.

Jack introduced Joshua as "Captain Barney, master of the good ship *Sidney*. He brought her in through that levanter ten days ago." Captain Wilder's hard blue eyes passed over the boy as indifferently as if he had been an insect, and Joshua's pleasure was immediately curdled.

Mr. Murray came out of the inner office at that moment and eased what was for Jack and Joshua an awkward situation by greeting both his guests cordially and announcing that they would walk up to the house.

The way led through more of the narrow, foul-smelling streets, until it left the town and began to climb. Mr. Murray and Wilder walked ahead, with Joshua and Jack close behind. Jack was chatting easily about affairs on the Rock but Joshua's attention was divided between Jack's remarks and snatches of conversation he could overhear from Mr. Murray and Wilder. The captain was making some indignant remarks about the Colonies in America and their never-ending political arguments with the Crown. Barney's whole being had been too intensively concentrated on seafaring for him to know or care anything about politics, and precocious as he was in some ways, he was even more ignorant of politics than the average youth of his age who remained ashore. The embargoes, of course, he knew about, since they had sent him to the Mediterranean instead of to England; but beyond the knowledge of that fact, he ignored them. When Wilder said something to the effect that the rebels in Massachusetts were traitors to the Crown who should swing from British yardarms, Barney heard him, and a good bit more in the same vein, and finally he asked Jack what it was all about.

"You tell me," Jack retorted. "You're fresh from there."

"Fresh from Baltimore. 'Tis a thousand miles from Boston. I know more about Gibraltar right now that I know about Boston."

They came presently to a gray stone house built where the steep slope of the talus joined the cliff. A terrace ran the length of it, with a waist-high parapet below which was a sheer drop. The tops of olive trees reached just below the parapet, and beyond and below them were the crowded roofs of the town.

Barney was paying no attention to the details of the house because his interest had been captured by the view that lay spread before his eyes. Beyond the town were the harbor and the bay, and all the shipping. The shore ran south to where the New Mole hooked around to the northwest like a long arm reaching out into the water, and in the curve of that hook, where the New Mole would shelter her from any seas that might be whipped up in the strait and the bay, lay the *Sidney,* hove down, and workmen crawling on her like ants on a giant caterpillar. Beyond the *Sidney* was the blue strait, and far off, across the strait, the misty shore of Africa.

"How do you like our view, Captain?" Mr. Murray asked, seeing the pleasure in Barney's face.

"Finest I ever saw," he replied with enthusiasm, thinking of the ships and not at all of aesthetics. "Why, you can stand right here and see the commerce of nations sail past your feet!"

"So you can," said the Englishman. "So you can. All that traffic into and out of the Mediterranean flows right through the gut. And most of it in British bottoms, too."

"And that gut controlled absolutely by our forces at Gibraltar, too," said Wilder, for the first time making a remark that was in any way responsive, however remotely, to anything Barney had said.

At that moment the front door opened, and an English butler stood aside. Mr. Murray marshalled his guests inside. The wide hall, Barney guessed, was furnished directly from England, but beyond that he paid little attention to it. Through a doorway he could see directly into the drawing room, where three ladies waited.

Wilder was greeted in a manner that showed he had been a guest there before. Mr. Murray, his arm through Barney's, led him in and introduced him to Mrs. Murray and his two daughters, Miss Susan and Miss Pamela, and for a moment he felt painfully conscious of his too-tight clothes. Miss Susan was a lovely thing for whom a man should be dressed in the best that tailors could produce. Her blue eyes, her golden hair, and her skin, so pink and white and delicate after the leathery hides he saw daily, left him breathless. Pamela was naturally darker, with gray eyes and brown hair and Barney immediately decided with distaste that she had been careless of her complexion and had become slightly sun-tanned. He turned his eyes back to Miss Susan.

"Jack has talked so much about you, Captain," said Mrs. Murray, "that we just had to have you up here and hear from your own lips how you brought your ship in through that levanter." Her gracious, friendly manner made him forget his appearance, and put him at his ease.

"The current brought me in, ma'am," he said.

"Ah," said Pamela, "but you had to catch the current. There was the decision to be made. Jack says your first officer tells it that he and the whole crew were terrified and wanted to run off before it. Truth to tell, Captain," she said with a merry twinkle in her gray eyes as she glanced at her brother, "Jack has been laying it on so thick that we—well, we thought the old boy . . ."

"Pooh for you!" said Jack.

The butler came to the door and announced luncheon. Over the table two very different conversations developed. Mr. Murray and Jack had heard Joshua's story and Captain Wilder was aggressively indifferent, so the three of them talked shipping and politics. The three ladies wanted Captain Barney's story from his own lips, and as he talked, they were plainly captivated. Under sympathetic questioning that came mostly from Pamela he had to relate his voyage in minute detail. As he talked, though, he heard the coarse-timbred voice of Captain Wilder speak, once, of treason in the Colonies. A little later Wilder referred to war between the Colonies and England. A few seconds after that there was a reference to "that lawless city of violence, Boston." Barney was finding it difficult to keep his mind on what was to him the most interesting subject in the world.

The other conversation veered away to more peaceful subjects, and Barney got ahead with his story.

Nobody was any more interested in Captain Barney's exploits than Captain Barney himself, but that would have been hard to guess from his diffident manner of telling it. His diffidence was in no degree due to modesty, for he was not modest. He never boasted, but neither did he ever underrate himself. Most likely it was due to the self-discipline he had shrewdly imposed upon himself when, as a small boy in a world of grown men, both Captain Chilton and Harry Dodge had raised the question whether he was cocky. The effect, however, was of modesty, and the ladies were charmed. For that matter, so was he. He had never before been a hero, and he wished Captain Wilder wouldn't spoil it by his renewed and frequent references to war, but there it was again—"war in the Colonies." All claptrap, of course.

As Barney talked, his eyes kept straying to Sue. She

smiled at him. Then she pouted. "Why must they be forever talking of war, Captain?" she asked him. "It is so wearisome. The Colonies aren't going to war with us, are they, Captain?"

"Hardly, ma'am. How could we? We haven't got a single warship. Not one. In fact, ma'am, we're more likely to fight among ourselves."

It was Pamela, though, who asked most of the questions about the voyage. Barney was surprised that a young lady should talk so much. To his way of thinking, until she knew a man well, it was hardly modest to talk so much. He finally realized that at least her questions were remarkably apt. His first clear realization of that fact came when she had brought him back from thoughts of war to the burial at sea. "Then I told 'em to decide if they would go ahead with me." He was looking at Sue when he said it, and he more or less consciously expected some sign that she understood the critical importance to him of that moment, but her blue eyes looked back at him without a change of expression until, seeing that he was regarding her intently, she gave him another of her melting smiles. It was the wrong response, and it left him deflated.

"Oh, Captain Barney!" Pamela exclaimed, "you must have gone all weak in the knees to leave such a decision to them!"

"Why, ma'am," he said, looking at her more attentively than he had done before, "it is surprising you should say that. My knees were so weak I could scarce climb the companion ladder." Until that moment he'd been so ashamed of that weakness that he would not have admitted it to a soul, but Pamela's ready understanding first surprised it out of him, and then made it seem natural and right.

Thereafter he talked less and less to Susan and more and more to Pamela. He soon discovered that her gray eyes had a surprising way of lighting up when she smiled, and he found it captivating. He set himself deliberately to make them light up.

Mr. Murray broke in on this pleasant pastime with a question.

"What is brewing in your country, anyway, Barney?" he asked.

"Brewing? Why, sir, nothing out of the ordinary, I'd say."

"Wouldn't you say that embargo by all the Colonies in defence of the one city of Boston was something out of the ordinary?"

"Oh, that! 'Tis not the first. 'Tis on that account, now, we're trading to the Mediterranean instead of to England."

"Captain Wilder thinks war is brewing between England and the Colonies. I trust you can set his mind at rest."

"I'll be in a bad way if war comes while my ship is hove down in a British naval base!"

"A lot of Colonials will be in a bad way," said Wilder with relish. "At least, their necks will be. The world knows how we handle traitors."

"I regret, my dear," said Mr. Murray quickly to his wife, "that I must return to the countinghouse. I suspect Captain Barney is impatient to return to his ship, too. He probably reckoned without knowing our leisurely habits. I'll be glad to have you walk down with me, Barney. Jack, you and Wilder can come at your leisure."

Mrs. Murray rose, and all at table followed her. Barney was smarting under Wilder's remarks but unwilling to start anything resembling a quarrel at his hosts' table.

Besides, he was too ignorant of the political situation to make an intelligent reply. And as Mr. Murray had guessed, he was impatient to return to his ship. He didn't trust that foreman.

Mrs. Murray asked him to leave the tavern at which he had taken lodgings and come stay with them while he was on the Rock. They would all, she assured him, be delighted to have him, and she promised that he would be much more comfortable and better fed. The invitation was enthusiastically seconded by all the Murrays.

"I fear you will spoil me for sea duty, ma'am," Barney said, "but that is a risk I will gladly take for the sake of the good company I will have."

CHAPTER ELEVEN

THAT EVENING AS JOSHUA DESCENDED THE WIDE STAIRWAY he could hear the ladies ahead of him in the drawing room. He was wearing his new suit, only just come from the tailor, and he was intensely anxious for it to do him credit. This was the first suit he had ever selected for himself; heretofore he had been so indifferent about his clothes that he had always been glad to have his mother select the materials. The costume was dignified to the point of severity, for he did not like foppishness, and when he had been examining fabrics, the tailor, showing him a lemon yellow that he recommended for the vest, had objected that the darker fabrics made him look older. That had settled it. He hoped earnestly that they were in good taste, but he felt his lack of experience in such matters.

The tar that had worked so deeply into all the crevices of his hands and around his nails during his years aloft had begun to come out during his weeks of command and since his luncheon with the Murrays he had rubbed them almost raw in his determination to remove the last traces of it. The club of hair that rested on the nape of his neck had been cleared of tar before he reached Gibraltar, and now it was tied with a wine-red ribbon that exactly matched the red of his coat. His tight-fitting breeches were dark blue, with silver buckles for his knees; his vest was a lighter but not a bright blue, and his stockings were white silk.

He was not an elegant figure, for all his pains. He was too stocky, too powerful and virile, to look elegant. His coat could not hide the thickness and power of his broad shoulders. His thighs and calves bulged with muscles developed in racing up the ratlines; but his brilliant eyes and friendly, mobile face with its air of recklessness, marked him as a lad of rare charm. And if he wasn't exactly elegant, certainly there was something about him of distinction as well as of charm; an air, a beguiling glance, a manner, lay like a rich velvet cloak over the contours of character that said plainly, Delight with me in my mirth but beware my wrath.

"You look most handsome, Captain," said Susan.

"Why, thank you, ma'am," he replied, immensely pleased.

"Sue, don't be forward," her mother admonished her. She looked at him. "But that costume does become you, Captain. Though I am going to call you Joshua."

"Why, ma'am, I'd like that vastly." He walked over to the hearth, where a fire burned briskly with the bright blue and green flames of wood saturated with sea salt—for the February evening was chilly. Susan smiled at him.

"Tell me some more about your boat, Captain," she begged.

Joshua looked at her in amazement. Lived all her life in a seaport, and didn't know the difference between a boat and a ship! "Why, ma'am," he said, "I guess I've told you about all there is to tell." He looked at Pamela. She was sewing quietly, having said nothing beyond the greeting she had given him when he had entered the room. He caught her eyes on him now, and he suspected there was a faint smile in their gray depths before she dropped them again to her work. He couldn't imagine Pamela asking such a fool question. His eyes searched Susan's face again. Just a pretty picture on an empty box, he decided. And when Pamela did start talking, drawing him out on this and that, he fell to studying her lively, mobile features in a way that was new to him. She was really much better looking, he decided, than he'd realized at first. Her brows were long and dark, and flared up slightly at the temples with the airy grace of the wings of a soaring gull. He studied her other features. A man with an eye for the lines of a ship, he thought, should have seen more in her face right from the first. Her nose was high-bridged and spirited, and delicately carved around the nostrils, and her lips had a fullness and at the same time a delicacy of line that he liked better the more he studied them. What a shame she'd let the sun mar her complexion! It was Susan's brilliant coloring that had first caught his eye, but color was all Susan had. Pamela had vivacity, and ever-changing expressions to fit her moods, and she had a grace and beauty and symmetry of line that Susan lacked entirely.

A few days later Captain Wilder was again a guest at the Murray's, this time for dinner. When he entered the parlor where the family was assembled, he found Joshua, Jack and Pam engaged in a lively three-cornered conversation, with Sue listening and showing a slight tendency to pout, and Mr. Murray tossing in an amused word now and then while Mrs. Murray worked placidly at a bit of embroidery. The captain spoke graciously to all present except to Joshua, to whom he made the most meager of bows, and Joshua's hackles immediately began to rise.

The butler announced dinner a few minutes later. The family and their guests were scarcely seated before Wilder took the conversational lead with a blistering remark about the army garrison on the Rock. The governor, he asserted, was a scoundrel, fit to govern nothing better than a pack of dirty colonials. All he could think of was to fill his pockets with gold. The magazines were nearly empty and His Majesty's warships could not restock there. "But after all, what can you expect of the army?" he demanded.

Jack, quick to divert him from the Colonies, was off on the garrison—a favorite subject of his. In fact, Joshua already knew Jack's figures by heart—only twenty-five hundred troops, and they disorderly and undisciplined; and it took four thousand just to man the defenses, with no allowance for reserves. This time, though, Jack surprised Joshua by adding a new thought.

"We'd be helpless if attacked by any real force," he said.

"What!" Wilder exclaimed. "With our warships in the harbor?"

"Our warships!" Jack echoed. "How many? Five! Five frigates! Fourth-raters! Only fourth-raters!"

"They're British, aren't they?"

Jack laughed. His good nature robbed his words of any sting when he said, "If that isn't a classic example of British complacency! Captain, only an Englishman would have said that—and no Englishman could appreciate it if he hadn't lived at such a crossroads of world trade as this is."

The captain did not smile, however. "Can you name such a real force as you referred to?" he demanded truculently.

"How about that mighty Armada the Spaniards are assembling all up and down their Mediterranean coast?"

"That's for Algiers. All Europe knows that."

"All Europe's been told that. That's why I doubt it. Captain, if you were preparing an Armada to attack the Algerines, would you tell them exactly what you were planning, months in advance, so they could assemble an army to welcome you?"

"No, but then I am no windy Spaniard."

"No, you are plainly an Englishman. Still, even an Englishman can be fooled, and my impression of the Spaniards is that they are more crafty than windy. Suppose, when that Armada is about ready to sail, Spain sends a declaration of war to London—the Spaniards would be in complete possession of this little wart on their coast line before a single ship could arrive with reinforcements from England. And can you name any one thing that Spain would rather do than recapture this Rock from us?"

The captain paused in his eating, laid down his fork, and sat back in his chair. "God bless my soul!" he exclaimed. He pondered, his brow corrugated. "You don't think the Spaniards would be smart enough to think up a scheme like that, do you?"

"I wouldn't call it smart at all. I'd call it elementary. And here we sit, utterly unprepared, and gamble the Rock and all it means to us, on our complacent belief that the Spaniards aren't smart enough to play an elementary little trick like that on us! It seems to me that makes us more stupid than you consider them!"

Joshua had conceived a powerful aversion for the arrogant captain, and it delighted him to see the long horse face so baffled. He's stupid, he decided. He was enjoying the moment immensely.

"It would, Jack," said Mr. Murray, "if the Spaniards could possibly work together on such a grand scheme without letting word of it leak out. You may be sure our ambassador and our secret agents in Spain are alert for such a contingency."

The captain took a deep breath and returned to his food. He was a stout trencherman, and it had taken a major assault to divert him.

Pam, apparently deciding the conversation had become too deep, set a course for shallower waters. In such shoal waters the captain floundered and soon ran hard aground. Pam revealed a great gift for whimsical, light-hearted humor, and Jack immediately followed her lead. They proved to be a very clever team, and with occasional remarks from Mr. Murray, they kept up a steady flow of frivolous, witty conversation. Joshua, delighted, managed a toss of his own now and then, but the captain ate in stony silence and Sue pouted as she ate, until the meal was finished and Mrs. Murray rose and led her daughters from the room.

The gentlemen settled down to their after-dinner conversation. The talk soon touched upon the Colonies. Captain Wilder remarked that the rebels in Massachusetts were traitors and should be swung from the yardarms of British warships. "Let me have my way with the dogs," he said, "and I'd soon put a stop to their riots."

"I don't agree with you at all," Mr. Murray said quickly, with a glance at Captain Barney. Joshua felt hot blood rising in him again, in spite of the distance between Maryland and Massachusetts, for Wilder had an insulting way of lumping all colonials together and speaking of them with the most galling contempt. Mr. Murray raised his voice and deliberately overrode an attempt by Wilder to take the floor.

"Englishmen have fought oppression for hundreds of years in order to establish their rights," he said. "It is an Englishman's hard-won right to have a voice in the making of the laws that govern him. I hope Englishmen will always fight for that right, wherever they live, all over the world. That is what the colonists are doing, and Burke and Pitt and the rest of our Whigs know that. It is the Tories, with their subservience to our despotic king, who are responsible for all the trouble. When the Whigs come back into power they will straighten it all out. This degenerate governor, here on the Rock, is just a sample of the corruption of the King's party."

"Sir," said Captain Wilder, "aren't you sailing dangerously close to disloyalty?"

"What would you say, Captain, of the barons who defied King John in 1215 and wrung the Magna Charta from him by show of their naked swords at Runnymede? Were they disloyal? Or were they champions of freedom of all Englishmen against the encroachments of a tyrannical king?"

"They were defending the God-given rights . . ."

"There are no God-given rights, Captain. Pardon me for interrupting you, but there are no God-given rights. Englishmen are not a chosen race. We enjoy those rights we have won by hard fighting, and we will continue to enjoy them just as long as we continue to fight for them, and no longer. But I interrupted you. You were saying . . . ?"

"I was saying that God-given or fought for makes no difference. This case is entirely different from Runnymede. Then it was the peers of the realm. Now it is a pack of lawless colonial rowdies who can't appreciate preferential treatment when it is given to them."

"What you Tories don't understand is, they don't want preferential treatment, and kindnesses, and bounties—all of which can be taken from them as capriciously as they are given. What they want is a government of laws, stable and dependable, and a voice in the making of those laws."

"In other words, sir, what they want is independence. Colonials, making their own laws! They have too much of that now, sir! We've been too liberal with the dogs. What you Whigs can't understand," declaimed the captain, getting red in the face, "is that we sent those colonists out there to provide a source of raw materials and revenue to the government and the merchants at home. That's what they are for, and, by God, sir, that's the purpose they have got to serve!"

"If you think, sir," Joshua exclaimed hotly, "that we are dogs for you to kick around, or slaves to serve your purpose and not our own, then you just don't know us!"

Captain Wilder whirled on Joshua, but before he could speak, Mr. Murray cut in quickly and forcefully, "There you have your answer, Captain! You may send Englishmen out to face the dangers and hardships of a great, wild continent, but if they are worth their salt, they soon demand a means for giving expression to that age-old passion for self-government that held sway in our island before the Norman tyrants came and clamped their tyranny upon us."

"Well, sir, if 'tis trouble they want, 'tis trouble they are going to get. We are well prepared to give it to 'em."

Mr. Murray hurled the stump of his cigar into the blazing embers with a vigor that betrayed more feeling than he had permitted his voice to reveal. "I think, gentlemen," he said, " 'tis time we rejoined the ladies."

The following morning Joshua stood on the up-turned side of the *Sidney* and watched the *Thetis* sail away to England, to get the supplies she should have been able to draw from the magazines deep in the galleries of the Rock. If we are going to have a war, he thought, I know which side I am going to fight on—if I can just get my ship home before the British seize her! His thoughts swung from his hosts to Captain Wilder and back to the Murrays. Which represented England? If the Murrays, then war was unthinkable. If Wilder, then it was inevitable. Mr. Murray had said the Tories were in power, and plainly, Wilder was a Tory. That was bad; but at the moment there was nothing he could do about it—except to drive ahead with all possible speed in the repairs of his ship.

CHAPTER TWELVE

BARNEY WAS HAPPY ON GIBRALTAR. THE PROSPECT OF A WAR, and of having his ship seized, was a cloud on the horizon and he never entirely lost sight of it, but he was not the man to shorten sail for a distant cloud. Life at the Murrays was delightful. Mr. Murray discussed politics with him, Joshua thought, as man to man. He had formed a most exalted opinion of his host's vast learning, and to have such a man spend so much time discussing politics with him pleased and flattered him. He even learned to take an intelligent interest in a subject that formerly he had scorned. The fact was that Mr. Murray was shocked at Joshua's ignorance of all subjects not related to seafaring, and he liked the boy so much that he took great pains to open his mind to a few others, but he was so diplomatic about it that Joshua never suspected his motive. And so he received a thorough drilling in Whig principles.

Mrs. Murray mothered him as he had not been mothered since he had gone to Alexandria at the age of ten, and he loved it. He had been too absorbed in seafaring to feel the lack of it, but now he revelled in it. His coarse cotton work stockings regularly turned up in her darning basket along with Jack's and Mr. Murray's silk ones. Sometimes she treated him as if he were a small boy, only, a moment later, to seek his opinion on matters of great importance to her. After his absolute authority afloat, it tickled him immensely to have her forbid him to spoil his appetite for dinner by eating any of the sweets that Sue, who was a pig about food, was forever smuggling and dividing with him.

Sue hung on his words and followed him about with her eyes. She pouted when he became absorbed in talk with Pam, and wept in secret.

Jack treated him exactly as if they were of an age when in fact there was a difference of ten years between them.

Pam, who was the youngest of the six Murray children —there being three sons still at school in England—kept him eternally guessing. She laughed and joked with him; she asked him innumerable questions about the work on the ship, and she astonished and delighted him by remembering what he told her and by her genuine interest and understanding. She darned a stocking or two for him occasionally. At times she assumed the condescending airs of a sophisticated woman of the world and having made him feel like a bumpkin in some small detail of drawing-room conduct, she laughed with delight and coquetted to make up. He was often exasperated with her, though never for long, especially after he finally concluded that if she didn't like him very much she certainly wouldn't give him so much of her time or show such genuine interest in his work. The fact was that he had spent too much of his boyhood at sea to have acquired the social polish to which his birth entitled him, and Pam was giving him the same sort of training for the drawing room that her father was giving him in politics, and doing it with such skill and subtlety that he never once guessed it.

Down on the ship, though, he was fighting a perpetual battle with Mr. McGregor and an entirely different kind of battle with the shipyard. With the yard, the battle was over the quality of the lumber supplied for the *Sidney*. With the carpenter foreman it was a battle of personalities in which lumber played only a minor role.

Only the best was good enough for the *Sidney*. Barney felt very keenly that in her original construction she had been given much less than the best, and he was determined that in her rebuilding she should have the best he could possibly get for her. When the contract had been drawn, Mr. Murray's advice, and perhaps some influence also, had enabled him to get much better specifications for lumber than he could have got otherwise, for the shipyard was a royal naval base and the Admiralty officers very naturally kept their best lumber for His Majesty's warships. The grading of lumber was not then standardized as it is now, but even so, there were specifications covering species and grades, though they were so loose that there was room for endless arguments among shipbuilders— and Captain Barney knew nothing about lumber. True, he knew a knot when he saw one, and he could tell a straight grain from a curly grain, and he knew the difference between sapwood and heartwood. Beyond that, though, when veteran ship carpenters fell to arguing about the merits of their favorite woods for resisting decay, all Barney knew was that whoever had been responsible for the selection of the lumber used in building the *Sidney* had cherished some mighty unsound ideas.

In this predicament he should have had the whole-hearted cooperation of the foreman. Instead, he feared that

Mr. McGregor would trick and befuddle him at every turn if he got the chance. Well, he thought, I slapped him down once. If I can bluff him into thinking I know as much about lumber as I do about how many strakes to remove at once—well, if I make him responsible for the lumber, as he should be, and then watch him and keep my mouth shut as much as I can, maybe he'll be afraid to try any tricks.

While he sweated over this problem he happened to see Noah Cotton, one of his sailors, examining the first lot of timbers sent him. In his very recent second-mate days he had known all the sailors intimately, and he knew that Noah had spent several years working in shipyards up and down the coast before he had taken to the sea. As a second mate it would have been only slightly out of order for him to discuss lumber with a sailor, or to pick his brains on the subject; but now a vast gulf separated them. For a captain to ask one of his seamen for expert information or advice was as unthinkable as it would have been for the seaman to volunteer it. However, he immediately decided upon a way to bridge that gulf. He walked up behind Noah, his footsteps noiseless in the dry sand. Noah was jabbing at the grain of the wood with the point of his case knife.

"Well, Noah, what do you make of it?" Barney asked him.

Noah spun about. For two years he and Barney had worked side by side alow and aloft and he was at least twice Barney's age, but now he had accepted the difference in their ranks so completely that when he suddenly found himself so close under his captain's eye he blushed and tugged at the brim of his tarred canvas hat.

"No offense, I hope, sir," he said. "I were just a-lookin'."

"Well, what do you see? Speak up, lad. What kind of oak is it?"

"Why, sir, it be some kind of furrin oak, seems like. I don't rightly know it, sir."

"See any sapwood? Any knots? Any curly grain?"

"No, sir. What I see be all clear, straight-grain timber. All heartwood."

"They may try to fox us, Noah, and I have too many things on me to watch every piece as it comes here. Suppose I told you to keep your eye on every piece of lumber sent me, could you spot any bad stock and call me right away?"

"Aye, sir," said Noah, grinning from ear to ear. "That I could, sir."

"Do that, then, and see you don't let me down."

"Aye, aye, sir. That I will, sir!"

Barney was about to turn away when he saw that Noah was struggling with an idea but very doubtful of the propriety of expressing it. "All right, Noah," he said, "what is it? Out with it!"

"I were just thinkin', sir, it do be a shame we can't get some chestnut oak, sir. It do be the best of all, I do believe, to stave off rot in a ship."

"We'll just have to make the most of what we can get," said Barney, wishing devoutly that he knew more about these foreign woods.

Noah was so proud of his appointment to inspect the lumber that he would undoubtedly tell his grandchildren about it—if he ever had any—but already Barney was wondering if he had done a good thing. The arrangement would by-pass Mr. McGregor completely—but hold on.

He could still make the old devil responsible; and the knowledge that he was being doubly watched might just possibly prevent tricks. In any event, his choice was made —and Noah would be faithful against any odds.

Thereafter, Barney often did reject timbers without Mr. McGregor's advice, and the foreman resented it bitterly. The old man knew lumber, but he was not giving this job the benefit of his knowledge, and Barney never regretted his choice of Noah. He often had occasion, though, in his arguments with the men of the shipyard, to wish that he had Mr. McGregor to back him up. He'd have fared better, without a doubt. As it was, he had to fight those battles alone.

Every time he rejected a piece of timber he ran headlong into some heated arguments, but they were always open and aboveboard and he never minded them, provided he got what he wanted. There were derogatory remarks about boy captains who thought they knew more than the experts, and about colonials who thought they were as important as the King's warships, but there was no bitterness in them and Barney fought them with gusto. And between arguments he made friends with the men he fought, and if they didn't always give him what he wanted, at least they generally did, and they learned to like and respect him for the man that he was, regardless of his youth.

With Mr. McGregor the battle was all very different. In an age that attached great importance to formal courtesy, the foreman stubbornly refused to show Barney the respect and courtesy due from a carpenter foreman to the captain of the vessel on which he was employed. And there was nothing open and aboveboard about Mr. Mc-

Gregor. He was sly and underhanded. The truth was that he was afraid of Captain Barney. He saw a fire in the boy's dark eyes, and he felt cold, hard steel in his character, and he had neither within himself. That was something, though, that he would never have admitted, even in his most secret thoughts, and he felt obliged to assert himself in order to prove that he was not afraid. The ways that he used were the ways of a coward and a bully. He smirked behind Captain Barney's back, and he indulged in winks and glances of contempt that set his carpenters to smirking. He made ambiguous remarks, but when Barney called him to account he always had inoffensive meanings to offer, though Joshua could see that the carpenters exchanged stealthy winks and grins. They were mostly the small, swarthy Scorpions, as the natives of the Rock were called, and they disliked the English and delighted in Mr. McGregor's tactics. And half the time the old man spoke in a tone of faint, sly disrespect—but through it all he was so cautious and so skillful that there was never anything definite on which Barney could hang an open issue. It was a wholly new situation to him, and very baffling and difficult.

And the worst feature of it was that if it went far enough it could seriously impair his hold on his crew, for sailors could hardly respect a captain who submitted to indignities from a carpenter foreman. The days passed, though, and the weeks passed, and Mr. McGregor gave no clear-cut provocation.

On the other hand, Barney had to admit—and he was immensely relieved when he could do it—the old man knew his business. He was an able ship-carpenter foreman with an intense pride in his work and a great contempt for shoddy carpentry, and his pride in his craft was enough to hold him to a high standard of performance. It was one thing to sneer at the Colonies, and to try in sly, under-hand ways to make a monkey of a boy captain; to slight his work would have been a different thing altogether.

The repairs progressed, therefore, against many spiteful little delays, and they were well done. Two whole new frames were built inside the hull, jamb up against the two rotten frames they were to replace; and when they were set and the planking was treenailed to them, the old frames were chopped out a bit at a time. Then all the defective planks on the starboard side were stripped off, one at a time, and replaced. Finally the ship was floated on the high tide, and turned about, and hove down on her other side.

One morning Captain Barney arrived at the ship half an hour late. Mr. McGregor was squatting on his heels under the stern, drawing a diagram in the hard sand with a pointed stick for the instructions of several carpenters who squatted around him. Barney climbed the ladder to the high side of the hull. Two carpenters were at work there. They had ripped off two strakes side by side and were starting on a third. They had not seen Barney come up the ladder and before they knew he was about he was upon them in such a fine fury that his stout right boot sent them rolling and tumbling down the curve of the hull, to bounce off the keel into shallow water.

This was the direct result of Mr. McGregor's persistent, sly insolence, and Barney knew it. "Mr. McGregor!" he roared. "Come up here!"

At that peremptory command, the foreman stood up and glared. "I'd have ye understand . . ." he started, and then, over the curve of the stern he saw that wide gap between Barney's feet. He glared around at the grinning carpenters. He could do either of two things. He could humble himself by admitting the fault, fire the men responsible (they had already fled as fast as their bruises would permit) and take whatever bawling-out the upstart boy chose to give him; or he could try to brazen it out. To humble himself before a beardless boy would be too bitter a pill; much too bitter. He hesitated.

"How many strakes do you propose to strip off at one time?" Joshua demanded. To his shame, his voice broke and ran up the scale like that of any other adolescent boy. He had thought he was long through with that embarrassment.

The carpenters snickered. That decided Mr. McGregor. He grinned insolently, "What frights ye, laddie?" he asked. "Feared o' fallin' through?"

"That's enough monkey business out of you. If you're a ship carpenter, you'll give me a straight answer. If you're not, I'll fire you where you stand. Now make up your mind, and be fast about it!"

To be fired for so grievous a fault in ship carpentry would be a disgrace he could never live down—for he had no union to back him up right or wrong and a man stood or fell on the quality of his work. The upstart boy had chased him out on a yardarm and was just about to saw it off. For what seemed a long time he gulped down his own spittle and sought frantically for a dignified way down off that yardarm.

"Well?" Barney goaded him.

"What is it ye want to know?"

"I don't stutter. You heard me. Answer or clear out!"

With bowed head the old man walked to the foot of the ladder and climbed it. He stood before Captain Barney shamefaced, and he endured a tongue-lashing for all the sly insolence that had prompted this final act of insubordination. It was delivered in a tone for all to hear, and it was a bitter dose for a gray-haired man to take from a beardless boy, but he took it.

"And now we'll have an understanding," Barney finished. "I'm the master of this ship and if you're to finish the job here, you'll treat me with the courtesy that is due my rank. Is that understood?"

"Yes, sir. It is."

It was the first time he had ever said *sir* to Joshua, but he said it now with conviction.

"Then get ahead with your work."

"Yes, sir," he said with vast relief. He scrambled swiftly down the ladder, seized a stout stick that lay on the sand, and went after his carpenters roaring violent threats against any man who scamped his work. The carpenters fled around the hull and Mr. McGregor chased them around and around, into knee-deep water and out again at every circuit, roaring his threats until he was exhausted. Barney watched the performance with a faint smile of contempt, while his delighted crew cheered and jeered.

His ascendency over his carpenters thus affirmed, Mr. McGregor flung down his cudgel and stood, panting, while the carpenters, with sly grins now for their foreman, went back to their work.

CHAPTER THIRTEEN

THE *Sidney* WAS AFLOAT AGAIN, AND CAPTAIN BARNEY WAS showing such impatience to be away that Pam looked at him with hurt eyes.

Spring had come up out of Africa, and the days were hot and the nights balmy. The people in the long, narrow limestone house built against the cliff had abandoned their drawing-room fire and spent their evenings in comfortable chairs on the terrace overlooking the town, the bay and the strait. Pam and Joshua sat a little apart, and for once Pam was not showing her usual interest in his affairs. Instead, she was trying to draw him on to another subject. And he was disappointingly unresponsive.

The moon was low in the west, and prodigal as always with her silver on the dancing water.

"Moonlight on a summer sea," Pam said. She waited a moment, and tried again. "We'll miss you when you are gone, Joshua."

"I'll miss you, too. You have all been mighty good to me—took me in a stranger and treated me like one of the family."

"You have seemed like one of us."

"I can't imagine what I'd have done without your father. I'd have been sunk but for his loan. And then Mrs. Murray and you and Jack and Sue. All of you."

"I can see that Papa was a help."

"Sometimes I wonder what I would have done if he'd refused me the loan."

"And of course, Mama did darn your stockings."

"Of course. She's been like a mother."

"And Jack, like a brother?"

"Of course."

"And Sue and I—sisters?"

"Certainly."

She sighed. "And now that you have sailed away and left us, we all miss you."

Joshua looked hard at her.

"Oh, yes, indeed we do. All of us."

"Now what on earth . . . ?"

"Oh, don't you know? Your mind and your heart have sailed away and left your body behind; just an empty shell of you. Where are you now, Joshua? In Nice, disposing of your wheat? In Alicante, laying in a cargo for your return voyage?"

"Pam! Am I as bad as that?"

"Truly you are."

He reached out impulsively and took her hand. "Truly, I am right here with you." He squeezed. "Feel that? Same old Joshua. I will never forget you, Pam. Honestly, I never will."

Pam sighed again. "That's a comfort," she said.

The ship was rerigged. She was all but loaded. Captain Barney sat down with Mr. Murray and Jack at the big table in Mr. Murray's private office and added the last of the bills to the running total they had been keeping as the weeks had passed. It came to a grand total of just over seven hundred pounds sterling—a large sum in that day and a huge one for Joshua, but with a steady hand he set his signature to the paper that bound his ship for its repayment.

Jack had to attend to some business for the firm in Nice and it had been decided two weeks ago that he would wait and sail with Joshua. "To collect a certain bottomry bond," Joshua had said with a laugh; but if he had actually thought Mr. Murray had so little confidence in him after their close intimacy for more than three months, he'd have been cut to the quick.

"Get yourself together, Jack," he said now. "I mean to get sail on her as soon as the last sack of wheat goes down her hatches." And that afternoon he served tea for the Murrays in his cabin. He was very proud of his spacious quarters, which seemed immense to him after the second mate's cubby he had occupied for so long, and he had had them scrubbed and painted and polished for the occasion. He was in uncommonly fine humor, for did he not have everything that a young man's heart could desire? The tea was a brilliant success, and when the Murrays, all except Jack, who was sailing with him, went ashore, Mrs. Murray kissed him on both cheeks and Mr. Murray wrung his hand hard and wished him all the success in the world. Pam lingered behind the others and when they turned to go down the gangplank she threw her arms around his neck, kissed him full on the mouth, and whispered, "Come back soon, Joshua!" Then she fled after her family.

From Gibraltar to Nice is about nine hundred miles.

The weather was warm and pleasant, with none of the wind that Joshua so ardently desired for feeling out his ship after the major operation her hull had undergone. He spread skysails and studding sails, and drove his crew hard for two days getting all standing and running rigging adjusted to his satisfaction; then, on the third day, he and Jack stood together on the poop deck in the pleasant spring weather and whiled the time away.

Jack still talked about that Spanish Armada, which must surely be ready to sail by this time. "The Moors," he said, "are Spain's ancient enemies. I grant you that—but only because they invaded and occupied Spain. Now the Spaniards have whipped them and driven them out. They haven't whipped us. We still occupy the strongest point on their coast—one of the best natural fortresses in the world. There's nothing they'd like better than to drive us off the Rock. Burn me, Josh—but I'd give a lot to finish up in Nice in time to go on with you to Alicante!"

When Captain Barney awoke the next day at dawn he felt immediately that the wind had freshened, and when he stepped out on deck the sea was thick with white caps. Mr. Barnes had just finished taking in the studding sails, but the staysails had not been touched and Barney kept them flying.

The wind continued to freshen, and the occasional bursts of spray that leaped over the weather bow grew more frequent. Barney began to feel out his ship after her long sojourn on the beach, and he had no intention of taking in more sail unless he had to. In another hour the whole forward half of the ship was continually smothered in huge fans of spray that drenched the deck and blew in long, smoking streamers down to leeward. The *Sidney* settled down to her work as if she loved it. As if, Joshua swore, she revelled in being once more afloat.

When Jack came on deck he looked about him with a wary eye. He had made many voyages between England and Gibraltar, but never had he seen a ship driven as this ship was being driven. He looked as Joshua, but that young man was aloof, withdrawn, utterly absorbed. Feeling shut out, Jack went down the companion ladder to the main deck and in the waist of the ship be backed up against the weather rail, his feet braced before him on the sloping deck, and gazed aloft. That vast mountain of canvas with the wind roaring and booming through it fascinated and disturbed him. Royals he was accustomed to, but skysails! And staysails, too, in such a wind! The day was glorious. The sky was the deep, deep blue of the Mediterranean, flecked with what Joshua always called "God's wash hung out to dry," but the wind was blowing half a gale.

He gripped a sheet. It vibrated like a plucked violin string, and it sang like one, too. All of those scores of lines —the halliards, the sheets, the stays—all of them, were playing tunes as they sliced the rushing wind, and all those tunes, from shrill to deepest bass, blended into one vast, deep-throated, rushing roar. Power! thought Jack; tremendous power! Can a mere boy ride such power?

Water streamed down the steep deck to the lee scuppers, racing whitecaps grabbed lingeringly, greedily at the lee rail, and one of them sloshed a ton or so of water aboard. Uneasily he glanced aloft again. A few sailors moved like monkeys far above his head. At the start of the voyage Joshua himself had spent much of his time where those sailors were now.

Mr. Barnes came along the deck and Jack tried to catch his eye, but the mate had eyes only for the ship. His set expression told Jack what he wanted to know, though; he was as anxious as Jack was about all that straining canvas and all those taut, humming lines.

A dollop of spray the size of an orange slapped the side of his head with a force that stung. It burst into his ear and drenched his shoulders, and he went aft, climbing the ladder to the dry poop deck. Joshua stood there, his back to the taffrail, his head thrown back, his brilliant dark eyes alight with a strange inner fire as they moved from sail to sail, from detail to detail of his splendid ship. Jack felt a little awed by his friend and scarcely dared to interrupt such dedicated concentration. To his surprise, Joshua gave him a flashing smile. "She's as good as ever, Jack," he said triumphantly. Jack felt unreasonably pleased, as if some unusual honor had been paid him.

At Nice, Joshua and Jack went to call on the consignees, the Vespucci Fratelli. The ancient room in which the two Italians received them, with its leaded windows and its high desks where clerks stood to handle huge ledgers, was not very different from others in which Joshua, as an overworked apprentice, had transacted business for Captain Drysdale.

The two Vespucci brothers received them with much ceremony, the elder paying them compliments in fluent English, the younger gabbling away in Italian, which, to Joshua, was incomprehensible. They were swarthy fellows who wore heavy velvet jackets with fur borders in May, and stank of rancid sweat like any hard-working sailor. When their love of ceremony had been satisfied, the younger became silent and the elder did the talking, though he interrupted himself frequently to translate for his brother. When Joshua proposed the addition of the seven-hundred-pound bond to the price of the wheat, the brothers were indignant. Discussing it between themselves in Italian, their eyes snapped and their hands flew in excited gestures and Joshua fully expected a flat refusal.

Jack interrupted to remark that during the three months the *Sidney* had lain at Gibraltar the price of wheat had advanced so greatly that the increase in the value of the cargo would more than cover the amount of the bond.

This bit of information appeared to pass unnoticed, but Joshua saw that the younger brother was glancing frequently at him. Suddenly, as if afraid they might be understood (as indeed they would, since Jack knew Italian) they retired to a corner and spoke for a few minutes in whispers. When they returned, their manner had changed. The younger was silent; the elder had become cordial again. He left the bond and inquired with interest about the damage to the ship.

Puzzled, but pleased by the change and ever ready to talk about the *Sidney,* Joshua told him something of the difficulties he had encountered. Jack, proud of his friend, told considerably more, until Signor Vespucci had the whole story. Finally, to Joshua's surprise, he reverted to the bond and accepted it readily; then, all smiles and compliments, and talking so volubly about what a wonderful young man Captain Barney was that neither of the young men could slip in a word edgewise, he ushered them out of the door.

"We didn't get that slick rascal's signature on that acceptance, Jack," Joshua said before they had gone a hundred yards.

"Burn me, Josh! You know, that monkey talked so fast, he talked us right out without it. Think it'll be all right? I'd feel mighty sheepish going back there for it now."

"We couldn't do that. We'll just have to go ahead and hope they'll pay up."

Jack took up lodgings ashore in order to get ahead faster with his business, and Joshua went about the unloading of the cargo. The facilities of the port were poor and the work dragged, but Joshua was not easy in his mind about that bond, so he was content for it to drag. The ten days allowed for payment passed, and the wheat was only half unloaded, so he called on the Vespucci Fratelli and inquired whether payment had been made. The Italian laughed in his face. "We will pay you for your wheat," he said, "but pay good monies to a fool who lends money to a mere boy? Pfui!"

"Are you telling me you intend to repudiate the bond?"

"Repudiate? What is there to repudiate? We signed nothing. We repudiate nothing."

"Your verbal agreement is nothing, then?"

"Ah, that? Pfui! A mere word, a little sound upon the air. Who can see it? Who can catch it? Pouff! It is spoken, it is gone!"

"So that's your way of doing business!" Joshua was too astounded to think of a more effective comment. Then, feeling the futility of argument, he added, "I'll see you in court; and in the meantime, you'll get no more wheat."

"We have half your wheat now, Signor Capitano, and until we get the rest, you will get no monies at all."

Seething, Joshua stalked out.

Aboard the *Sidney* he ordered the hatches closed, but as he paced the deck in a rage he knew how helpless he was. Legal action would be futile; the Nicean courts would support their fellow townsman.

A boat came alongside and hailed to come aboard.

"No!" Barney roared.

"Tell the captain," Joshua heard a man say in fairly good English, "that I am from His Excellency, the Governor of Nice, in the matter of the wheat."

"Tell him to come aboard!"

The messenger wore the uniform of a lieutenant in the army. He invited Joshua to accompany him to a conference with the governor. Barney realized that the governor could not have heard of the matter except from the Vespucci Fratelli, in which case, he would have a very one-sided account; and it seemed important to put his own side of the argument before him, so he readily agreed to go.

The officer led him through the city to the governor's palace and up a broad stairway to a huge room. Soldiers in brilliant uniforms stood at attention all down both walls, and as he advanced, Barney could not fail to be impressed by the power of the man he was calling upon.

On a dais at the far end of the room stood a great, elaborately-carved and gilded table, and behind it, in a throne-like chair, sat the governor, his head bowed over a document that lay spread before him, his fingers toying idly with its corners.

When Barney was near enough to see how dirty the governor's fingernails were, he was positive he saw the bushy brows lowered furtively, as if the fellow had been watching his approach, and he immediately guessed that the governor was uncommonly anxious to make an impression upon his caller. When he stopped at the table, the governor remained bent over the document. Barney waited a moment; then, exasperated at such play acting, he spoke. "You sent for me, Excellency?"

The governor raised his head. "You are the master of the ship *Sidney?*" he asked.

"I am, sir."

"Your cargo is consigned to Vespucci Fratelli?"

"It is, sir."

"And at an agreed price?"

"At an agreed price, yes—but subject to a bond also agreed upon."

"A bond for seven hundred pounds, in addition to the price, for which you have no signature? I ask you, Capitano, would you have me believe so fantastic a story as that?"

"I would. It is true."

"Would you cheat two of my loyal subjects?"

"Would two of your loyal subjects cheat me, Excellency?"

"Do you stand there and defy me? You, a mere apprentice boy? Me, the governor of Nice? I command you, sir, deliver your wheat or dread the consequences!"

"I will deliver the wheat when the bond is paid, not before."

"*Now,* I say! *Now!*" The governor leaned forward and beat with his open palm on the table for emphasis, his voice rising in anger.

"So this is Nicean justice!" Barney exclaimed furiously.

"I am too easy with you!" the governor screamed. "Why do I waste my time with you when I could put you to the torture? I am too soft-hearted, but do not try me too far! Capitano, deliver the wheat or dread the consequences!"

"Don't forget that I am a British subject, Excellency," Captain Barney retorted. "If you go too far with a British subject, it is you who will dread the consequences!" Seething, he turned and stalked out.

The governor's voice, shrill with rage, followed him, but as he spoke now in Italian, Barney could no longer understand him. As he started down the stairs, an officer came behind him and snapped a command to the soldiers in the lower hall, and as Joshua went on down, they met him with fixed bayonets levelled at his belly. With no need for words they directed him along a hallway that ran behind the stairs into quarters that rapidly became squalid, until at last they came to a massive, iron-studded door. Barney was thrust through the doorway into a dirty cell in which a heap of mouldy straw covered a pile of old filth in one corner. The door clanged shut behind him, and the key screeched in the rusty lock.

Joshua fell to pacing the cell—two paces one way, about face, two paces back again. Mr. Barnes had heard the messenger say that the governor of Nice wished to see him; would Mr. Barnes have sense enough to go to Jack for help? He had not the slightest idea where Jack was, or even that he was still in Nice. In fact, by this time Mr. Barnes, also, might be in prison. If a governor would seize the captain, would he boggle at a mere mate?

Jack could get him out, if Jack knew; but weeks might pass before Jack learned—if indeed he ever did learn.

Reflection now began to replace anger, and with reflection came a sick feeling of futility and failure.

Two paces, about face, two paces back again. If the governor were reckless enough to go this far, there was no knowing how much further he would go. There was

no reasonable stopping place, no safe stopping place
short of a completely silenced tongue. If the governor
were smart enough to pay Jack's bond and send him on
his way, satisfied, he and the Vespucci Fratelli could share
the ship and the cargo; and if England did go to war with
the Colonies, who then would ever come asking questions
about young Captain Joshua Barney?

Footsteps sounded along the stone floor of the corridor,
the small shutter that covered the barred window in his
door was opened, and the eyes of the officer who had
brought him from his ship appeared at the opening. He
was truly sorry, he said, to see the captain in such a
plight. His Excellency sent word that Captain Barney
would be released as soon as he agreed to deliver the wheat.

"Tell him I will deliver the wheat when I am once
more on board my ship," Barney snapped at him.

The officer departed. Half an hour later the turnkey
came and unlocked the door, and Joshua strode forth.
Aboard the *Sidney* again, he was relieved to find that his
cargo had not been tampered with. He went at once to
his cabin and wrote a note to the governor stating that
he did not feel bound by a promise that had been forced
upon him, and that he would not deliver the wheat until
Mr. Murray had been paid. He did not expect a reply that
day, as it was then near sunset; but the next morning early
he saw four boats, all loaded with soldiers, putting off
from a pier and heading straight for the *Sidney*. His crew
crowded to the poop deck and begged permission to arm
themselves with capstan bars and marlinespikes and bat
them down as fast as they came up the side. "They'd turn
the guns of the fort on us, lads," Barney told them. "We
can't meet them with force. They have too much of it.

175

And I am not going to run off and leave the wheat I have already delivered."

The same English-speaking officer came up the ladder.

"I have orders, Capitano," he said, "to warp this ship up to the pier, break open her hatches, and remove her cargo."

"I can't stop you. You have the greater force. But I call your attention to the British flag over your head. It is not a good flag to trifle with. If you insist on taking my ship by armed force, I will have to report the matter to the proper officers of His Brittanic Majesty's government."

"Oh, but Capitano, we have no intention of taking your ship by force."

"And if I resist you, then?"

"Oh, but I must carry out my orders!"

"But if I resist?"

"Then I would be compelled to use force."

"That is all I need to know. I am surrendering my ship to armed force, but you will hear more about it. And I am leaving my flag flying, so that you can not forget to what flag this violence is done."

He turned to his mate. "Mr. Barnes! Disembark the crew!"

Captain Barney went over the side with his crew, and pulled to the *Scarab*, the British vessel nearest him in port. He boarded her, introduced himself to her master, Captain Larrabee, and explained his situation. He then asked if he might lodge his men aboard the *Scarab* during the emergency, and received a cordial assent.

From the *Scarab*, Joshua went ashore and hunted up Jack's lodgings, where he found that young man still sleeping. He whacked him vigorously on the rump.

"Uh! You sailors!" Jack grunted, opening one sleepy eye. "Burn me, Josh, can't you let a man get his sleep?"

"Would you like to take over my ship in payment of your seven hundred pounds?"

"Eh?" Eyes wide now, Jack sat up in bed. "What's up, Josh?"

"A gang of pirates have seized my ship and are even now unloading her. Under armed guard."

"My lungs and liver! Right in the harbor?"

Joshua told him the story.

"The bloody pirates! What you going to do, Josh?"

"Where's the British ambassador to this stinking sink-hole?"

"Let me think a minute." Jack swung his legs over the side of the bed. "Six o'clock! Burn me!" He yawned. "Nice belongs to the kingdom of Sardinia."

"That island?"

"Same name. But it's a lot more than that. The capital is at Torino. Our ambassador there is Sir William Lynch. Good man. Very good. Nice trip. I'm all finished up here. Go with you."

"Fine. But get yourself together. You speak this monkey-talk. I'll leave all arrangements to you."

Jack went to the door and bellowed down the stairs until his landlady put a touselled head out of her door, when he ordered breakfast for two and in a hurry; then started dressing rapidly.

In Torino, which they reached after a plodding three-day journey on muleback, they went at once to Sir William Lynch. "Sir," said Captain Barney, "I have to report as highhanded and villainous a piece of piracy against the British flag as ever was committed on the high seas."

The diplomat's eyebrows shot up, and he gave Joshua close attention; then promised immediate action.

"He'll get action, too; you can count on that," Jack said as they left.

Three days later a note came to Joshua stating that the matter had been settled, and he could return to Nice and collect what was due him. Very skeptical at such speed, he handed the note to Jack. "What do you think, Jack?" he asked. "Is he just getting rid of us? No man could have gone to Nice and back in this time."

"You can depend on anything Sir William tells you."

"But Jack, three days!"

"If his Sardinian Majesty tells Sir William he has dispatched orders to the governor, you could go with the messenger and it would be all right. Don't forget, the king that appointed him can fling him into jail as quick as he flung you. And the king of Sardinia isn't looking for trouble with England—you can lay to that."

The weather had been dry and the road was deep in dust, and Jack and Joshua were sore and blistered from their unaccustomed mode of travel. The journey seemed interminable, and both young men were in a bad humor —Joshua because Jack was so slow, and Jack because Joshua was so impatient. "Anybody'd think it was a sweetheart you were hurrying to, instead of a bloody old ship!" he blurted at last.

Joshua laughed. "I'm sorry, old fellow," he said. "Anyway, we're almost there."

As a matter of fact, they were then just about six or seven miles outside of Nice. Ahead of them, drawn off the road, they saw several magnificent carriages and beautiful teams, with grooms in gorgeous liveries standing at their heads. A number of brilliantly-dressed gentlemen stood at the side of the road. As Joshua and Jack advanced on their mules, the contrast between the sleek horses and carriages and the mules, plastered with sweat-caked road dust, was something to see.

The gentlemen advanced afoot to meet them.

"Blast my eyes!" Joshua exclaimed. "Jack, that's the governor!"

"Of course!"

They drew rein, sitting as lightly as possible on their blisters. Before them, in the deep, powdery dust, the governor, his head bared, bowed deeply. His expression was a comical study in fear, anxiety and shame.

"Most honored Capitano Barrr-nay," he said, "we crave your pardon most humbly for any inconvenience you may have suffered. We assure you that the scoundrels responsible for your inconvenience are now being most thoroughly punished. We implore you, tell us what we may do, that we may satisfy you completely."

Joshua's first impulse was to laugh, but he restrained himself. It was too much like kicking a man when he was down. He glanced at Jack and got a wink from a merry blue eye, and he grinned happily in return.

"See that the bond is paid to Mr. Murray as agreed," he said. "See that I am paid for my wheat. Pay the *Scarab* for lodging my crew, and pay Mr. Murray and me the expenses of our trip."

"Yes, Capitano, it shall be done immediately."

"See that it is." Joshua was about to ride on when his

eye fell upon the magnificent carriages that had brought the governor and his retinue to the meeting. He reined in again and turned to Jack.

"Come to think of it, Jack," he said, "we've sat these raw-boned brutes about long enough. 'Tis high time we rode in a carriage."

"Right, old boy," said Jack with the most radiant smile Joshua had seen on his face for several days. They swung stiffly to the ground.

"We'll just take that carriage of yours," Joshua said, tossing his reins to the governor.

"By all means, Capitano. I am mortified that I myself did not think of it."

Joshua found the *Sidney* still at the pier, her hold empty. While he stood on the poop deck talking to Jack, a messenger arrived and with much servile bowing and scraping, announced that he had come to pay all charges. Joshua presented his bill and it was paid without a murmur. And while he was still counting the money, the governor himself appeared in the doorway of the cabin. Joshua would not be interrupted until he had finished, and the governor stood respectfully at one side, his broad-brimmed hat in his hand, until the counting was completed. Then he bowed deeply and asked what payment would be required to satisfy the noble capitano for his anxiety and inconvenience.

To Joshua the proposal smacked somehow of bribery, and he showed his indignation plainly. The governor looked incredulous but instead of being offended, he astonished Barney by looking distinctly pleased.

"Then, noble Capitano," he murmured, "may I have your signature to that effect?" and like a magician pulling a rabbit out of a hat, he whisked a paper from a pocket in the gorgeous coat. It was in Italian, and while the governor could easily have translated it, Joshua did not trust him and sent for Jack to come and translate for him. It stated merely that Captain Barney, master of the ship *Sidney*, had received full indemnity for all inconvenience caused him.

Joshua signed it, and the governor, with a glance that looked remarkably like contempt, vanished through the doorway with a speed vastly different from his usual deliberate manner.

"Well, old boy," Jack asked then, "how much did you get out of him for damages?"

"What do you mean, damages? He paid for the wheat, and your bond, and our trip, and board for my crew."

"Sure. Sure. But you also signed a release for all anxiety and inconvenience caused you. What did you get for that?"

"The dirty dog wanted to pay for that. I told him indignities to the British flag could not be measured in pounds sterling."

Jack looked even more incredulous than the governor had looked a few minutes earlier. "Don't tell me you refused to collect damages!"

"What do you mean, Jack? Of course I did."

Jack collapsed in a chair. "Swizzle me!" he exclaimed. "Burn me down! Josh, I thought you were a smart lad, but I swear you need a nurse!"

CHAPTER FOURTEEN

CAPTAIN BARNEY'S ORDERS REQUIRED HIM, AFTER DELIVERING his wheat at Nice, to sail westward again for about five hundred miles to the Spanish port of Alicante and there to lay in a cargo of wines, silks and olive oil. Jack had completed his business in Nice, and he was agog to get on down to Alicante, for he knew that a part of the great Armada had been fitted out there and he hoped to see it before it sailed. In fact, he cherished a secret hope that while Joshua bargained with the Spaniards for a cargo he would be able to get some clue as to whether the Armada really would attack Algiers, for on that score he was stubbornly unsatisfied—though he had stopped talking about it.

Four days out of Nice, Joshua headed the *Sidney* into the triangular Bay of Alicante. He and Jack stood, as usual, on the poop deck.

"That bloody African sun!" Jack complained as the ship went about and the poop deck lost the shade it had been receiving from the mizzen sails. "It'll cook our brains, Josh." He dropped down the ladder to the main deck, where shade could still be found, and Joshua, remarking that he would call it a Spanish sun rather than African, followed him.

The lazy breeze, however, was probably African, for it blew from the south and it barely filled the sails. The *Sidney* loafed her way indolently between the converging shores of the bay.

There was not a ship to be seen.

"Gone!" Jack exclaimed in dismay. "Josh, it could be at Gibraltar right now! We won't find out what's happening on the Rock till we get there!"

"Oh, rats, Jack! Your father knows. Depend on it." He ducked his head and wiped his sweating face on his shirt sleeve.

A pilot boat ghosted out to meet them. As she came abeam, her sheet was slacked and the two vessels drifted side by side while an officer standing in the stern of the smaller one spoke in Spanish. Jack replied and translated, his face lighting up with relief and pleasure as he talked.

"He says some of the ships of the Armada did fit out here but this bay is much too small and they have assembled from all ports in the Bay of Cartagena before sailing for Algiers. . . . He says it isn't quite ready to sail; needs a few more transports. . . . Josh, he says you can get a mighty good charter fee for carrying troops and supplies."

"Tell him this is a merchant ship and we are here to lay in a cargo of wines and silks and olive oil."

Jack spoke again . . . "He says His Most Christian Majesty, Charles III, has no desire to constrain the shipping of a friendly power, but all warehouses and trading centers of his Mediterranean coast are closed to trade until after the Armada has sailed. He says you may depart in peace and go where you will; but His Most Christian Majesty would pay you most handsomely for the use of your ship."

"What about it, Jack? Isn't England neutral?" Joshua was already tingling with excitement at the prospect of taking part in a great military expedition, but after all, he had a duty to his owner.

Jack put the question to the officer, and reported back that already at least a hundred British and colonial ships had been chartered and were even then laden and ready at Cartagena. Only a few more ships were needed; and as for friendly relations, he did not think infidel Algeria cut much ice among the Christian nations of Europe.

Joshua luffed his ship and began the slow business of tacking out to sea against that faint southerly air.

"That monkey could be telling the truth about why the Armada assembled at Cartagena," Jack said, "but this bay would hold a lot of ships and it is a fact that Cartagena is a full day's sail closer to the Rock. And further from Algiers."

"Forget it, Jack," Joshua laughed. "You're hipped on the subject."

" 'Tis not your family that's on the Rock."

"I can't feel much difference between them and my own. Forget it."

"I know you think I'm a zany, Josh, but how would you feel if you found yourself a part of an Armada bound for the Rock?"

"Rest in peace, Jack. Rest in peace. If that Armada turns west out of Cartagena, we'll slip away from the other ships after dark and carry word to the Rock. The *Sidney*'ll outrun anything they have."

"With a couple of hundred Spanish troops aboard?"

"We'll fill the officers full of rum. Gag 'em and tie 'em hand and foot while they're drunk. Deliver 'em to the garrison to prove our story. Now forget it. To Cartagena we go, to help His Most Christian Majesty against the infidels. And to fill our money chest with Spanish gold."

A glance at the huge, square bay of Cartagena spoke eloquently of the reason for assembling the Armada there instead of at Alicante. It was several times as large; yet it was barely large enough to contain the Armada. The two young man gazed in a silence that was broken presently by Jack. "Never before in the history of the world, I do believe, has such a force of ships been assembled in one place!" He was a graduate of Oxford, and rather fancied himself as a historian.

The *Sidney* steered slowly into a mile-wide lane that opened through the center of the ships. Jack and Joshua tried to count them, but there were ships beyond ships, and their masts and spars made a wintry, leafless forest that defied computation.

Once more a pilot boat came off to them, and a customs officer hailed in understandable English. His Most Christian Majesty, Charles III, would like to charter this magnificent ship in a righteous crusade against the infidels of Algeria.

Barney, tingling to the tips of his fingers and toes, yet held back and sought to drive a hard bargain. "Use my unarmed ship in a war?" he exclaimed in mock alarm. "Suppose I lose her to enemy action?"

"We will indemnify you against such loss, Capitano. The enemy has no navy and I am sure we can trust you to remain beyond the range of his shore batteries, so we feel safe in our offer of indemnity. But I am not empowered to deal with you. I can only extend you a most cordial invitation to come aboard, and after I have directed your splendid ship to a mooring I will take much pleasure in escorting you to the proper authorities."

Joshua went. When he returned two hours later he was fairly prancing with delight. "Buckets of gold, Jack!" he exclaimed. "Buckets of gold!"

"As captain, don't you share in those buckets of gold?"

"Oh, sure. Sure. And we sail within the week!"

The *Sidney* was speedily warped up to a pier, and into her empty holds the cargo began to flow in solid streams on the backs of long lines of sweating stevedores.

"Spaniards never moved so fast since Noah," said Jack gloomily. "Or before him, for the matter of that."

Now the loading of a ship is beneath the notice of a captain, and Joshua had some idle time on his hands. "Let's go ashore, Jack," he said. "See the town."

Ashore, they wandered in the narrow, twisting streets of the ancient part of the town that lay on the strip of level land about the harbor. Garbage and ordure flung from doors and windows drew vast swarms of flies and reeked and rotted and stank in the sun. It was worse than Gibraltar—much worse.

"Most likely built about the time Romulus and Remus were being suckled by that old she-wolf," said Jack, "and not cleaned since."

Hostile glances met them as they left the water front behind.

"See what I mean?" Jack said. "These monkeys hate us

186

because we hold the Rock. There's nothing they'd like better than to slit our throats."

"They give me the creeps," Joshua replied, and a moment later he added, "Isn't that Captain Johnston yonder?"

It was indeed that same captain who had sent Barney to the Murrays nearly four months earlier, and he greeted them with evident relief.

"Reinforcements, by Godfrey!" he exclaimed. "I've been here a month and this is the first time I've been so far from the water front. Looks like the further I go, the more unfriendly they get!"

They stood, mopping their faces, and then, with a defiant impulse they turned into a tiny *cantina* before which they had chanced to stop. Its walls were of huge stones from which the mortar had largely disintegrated, but the stones remained in place by virtue of their size. The doorway was so low that they had to duck to enter, but it was cool and pleasant after the sun's heat, and it smelled of wine and garlic and sweat and dampness. There was not a window in it and the only light came from the doorway. There were only four tables and the three nearer the door were occupied. They took the remaining one, and settled down thankfully on the straight, hard chairs. As their eyes became adjusted to the dim light, they could see the hostile glances turned on them by the piratical, black-bearded men at the other tables. They were served by a woman so ancient that Joshua asked Jack if she, also, must not have been there along with Romulus and Remus and the she-wolf, but Jack ignored her. He was eager for details of the Armada. Captain Johnston said he had been swinging to his anchor, all laden and ready to sail, for over a month. "And I don't care if I stay a year," he added, "just so these monkeys pay me what my contract calls for. I'll make more'n I'd make tradin'."

As to the size of the Armada, though, he was uncertain. "You hear so many tales, you just don't know which of 'em to believe. Allowin' for considerable exaggeration, I'd say about twenty-five thousand troops; maybe less. Not more. Four hundred ships, right around there. Pretty near one hundred of 'em warships. Three hundred merchantmen will carry supplies for twenty-five thousand men for a long time, seems like.

"But it's bound to be a bust. There's quarrellin' amongst the generals and the admirals. The king's gone an' put an Irishman, General O'Reilly, in command of the troops, an' the army's mortally insulted. They'll throw away the war before they'll take orders from that Irishman. You'll see."

That afternoon when Joshua and Jack returned to the *Sidney* they found her main deck crowded with Spanish soldiers and a group of four officers on the poop deck. Joshua knew that he was to carry soldiers as well as supplies, but he was again surprised at the speed with which the Spaniards were moving. He stood at the gangplank and barked an order at the soldiers who packed the deck. "Attention!" Not a soldier knew the meaning of the word, but one of the officers on the poop deck spoke in Spanish, and the soldiers made a lane for Joshua and Jack to the poop-deck ladder.

At the head of the ladder the same officer greeted them with a courtly bow and introduced himself by a long string of names of which Joshua caught only two clearly

—Carlos and Sanchez, or "Sancheth," as the Spaniard pronounced it. Much impressed by the courtly grace and dignity of that bow, the long string of names and the captain's evident good breeding and unmistakable patrician appearance, Joshua did his best to emulate the bow and introduced himself as Captain Joshua of Baltimore in the Colony of Maryland Barney, Master of the ship *Sidney*. He was on the point of introducing Jack as Señor Jack of Gibraltar Murray, but remembered just in time how bitterly the Spaniards hated the British hold on Gibraltar, so introduced him merely as "My friend, Mr. Murray." He was sorry to let Jack down in that fashion, but it was the best he could do on such short notice.

The Spaniard's face was grave but Joshua fancied a twinkle of amusement sparkled in the brilliant dark eyes and he wondered just how big a fool he had made of himself. In the next moment, he found out.

Speaking excellent English, the captain introduced a major and two lieutenants. The major was haughty and indifferent, and Joshua disliked him at once. He spoke to the captain, who translated to Joshua: "The major commands me to inform you that he will take your large stateroom for himself. The two lieutenants and I will take your smaller staterooms. Our men will remain upon your main deck, as the weather is too hot for them in the hold."

Joshua was always erect, but now he imparted a ramrod stiffness to his spine in order to gain a more imposing height than his sixteen years had given him.

"Tell the major," he snapped, "that I will continue to occupy my stateroom, together with my guest, Mr. Murray. You gentlemen may dispose yourselves among the other staterooms. Your men may remain upon the main deck except when my crew needs the space for working the ship, when they will have to go into the steerage and cargo holds."

Joshua was expecting a flush of anger but instead he saw clearly that a delighted smile flashed briefly across the captain's face before he turned gravely to the major and translated. Anger flamed in the face of the major, however, and even in the faces of the two lieutenants, and torrents of eloquent Spanish poured from their lips. The captain turned again to Barney.

"I am commanded to inform you that this ship is under charter to His Most Christian Majesty and subject to orders of the army."

"So it is. But read the contract. It states clearly that I am to transport troops and supplies to Algiers but it says nothing about the disposition of either troops or supplies. The master of the ship is in supreme command. I will do what I can to make you comfortable short of giving up my own quarters."

Again the captain translated, and again there was heated language, but it ended when the major, with a venomous glance at Barney, stalked haughtily off the poop deck and off the ship.

The captain turned to Joshua, a distinctly pleased expression on his face.

"Very well, sir," he said. "I put myself and my two lieutenants in your hands."

"Where's the major going?" Joshua asked. He was decidedly uneasy about his bluff and that parting glance promised him nothing good.

"Back to the ship to which he was assigned. He had quarters on it but liked yours better. In my years in the army I have learned to sleep where night finds me, and I see plainly that you are a man after my own heart. Do with me as you will."

Joshua had found himself warming to this courtly young man, and those last words settled the matter. Here was a friend he could take to his heart.

"You may have my first officer's stateroom," he said. "Your lieutenants may have the other two staterooms. They are not commodious but they are adequate."

He was not accustomed to using such words as "commodious" and "adequate" and he was pleased with himself for finding them in his vocabulary. Must have learned 'em from the Murrays, without a doubt.

The Armada was to sail on the tide at sunrise, and when Captain Barney came on deck the sun's rays were already touching with glory the few wisps of cloud overhead.

Sails were breaking out on the warships, which were grouped near the mouth of the bay, and the silhouettes of men moving aloft were black against the pearly sky.

The sun glinted redly on the waves beyond the mouth of the bay, and a great gun boomed from the flagship. The crews of three hundred merchant ships sprang aloft. Capstans clanked. Anchors were catted. Sails took the breeze and were sheeted home.

This, thought Joshua, is not just a loose collection of ships, each to go its own independent way. This is a single striking force, aimed like a javelin in the hand of one man. And I am a part of it.

In two columns the warships sailed out of the harbor, the stately ships of the line in the lead, the frigates next, then the galeasses, and the xebecs last of all. Jack had joined Joshua on the poop deck, and as the first warships left the bay, he had watched them with his glass, saying nothing, but when he saw them head into the rising sun, he telescoped the glass and tucked it under his arm. Joshua, watching him, laughed. "Burn me down, Jack," he said, "but I do believe you're disappointed to be proved wrong!"

Jack grinned and shook his head. "Thank God this force is not for the Rock!" he said fervently.

CHAPTER FIFTEEN

BARNEY'S FRIENDSHIP WITH SANCHEZ RIPENED SWIFTLY. HIS English blood and American training made him more reserved, and the Spaniard's frank expressions of warm regard sometimes took him by surprise but always pleased him, and he responded in kind. Sanchez was about Jack's age but with Jack he was always gracious, though more reserved—more correct and formal.

"Captain Joshua of Baltimore in the Colony of Maryland Barney!" he said before that first day was done, threw his arm over Barney's shoulders, and laughed with delight. Joshua laughed with him.

"Let us discard formalities, you and I, my valiant friend," he said. "Call me Carlos. It is the name by which I am called in my family. How do your friends call you? Joshua?"

"Some of 'em. Some of 'em call me Josh. Take your choice, Carlos."

"Josh! Heaven forbid! It is a harsh sound. It grates upon my ear. Barney has a pleasing sound. I shall call you Barney, my valiant friend, and you will call me Carlos."

With Joshua, Carlos was often confidential; never with Jack. But as Jack spent a good part of his time with the lieutenants, who spoke no English, Joshua had ample time to draw Carlos out and satisfy his curiosity about the quarrel in the high command.

The Spaniards were deeply offended by O'Reilly's appointment. It was, they felt, a wholly unmerited insult, an unbearable slur. "When one's forebears have commanded fighting men in the service of one's country for a thousand years," Carlos said, his voice quivering with suppressed emotion, "one does not take kindly to being pushed aside in favor of an upstart foreigner—a mere count. A mercenary of Ireland to command a grandee of Spain! We fight for our country when it is necessary. At other times we manage our estates. We do not go about the world, hiring out as mercenaries. Our General Romana is very bitter. So are we all—very bitter. His forebears fought the Moors with great distinction for a thousand years until we finally hurled them back to Africa. He has sworn that he will put O'Reilly in his place. Why is that execrable man not in the service of his own country? He is an adventurer."

"My country," said Barney, "is a new country where men started all over again a hundred and fifty years ago. We give more thought to what a man is and what he can do than we do to his ancestors. When you give so much weight to General Romana's ancestors, aren't you putting your Armada under the command of men who have been dead for hundreds of years?"

Carlos gave Joshua a startled glance. "My friend," he said slowly, "you do have the most disconcerting habit of getting to the heart of a matter in a few words. And yet, it is not so simple as that." And he would say no more about the quarrel that day.

On the first day of July the Armada arrived at the Bay of Algiers and saw the city it had come to conquer. It lay upon the west bank of the bay, its whitewashed masonry buildings rising right out of the water and climbing in tier upon tier up the slope of the land. Waves washed the foundations of its waterside buildings, and small boats were moored to stout iron rings set in the walls.

The bay was an almost perfect semicircle not quite ten miles wide at its mouth, and from its curving shore the land rose in fertile, rolling hills cut by many small valleys and covered with fields of waving grain, with pastures, vineyards, olive groves and orchards. Dense stands of trees marked the winding courses of the little Xarac River and of other, smaller streams that flowed into the bay. It was a fertile, prosperous land and would have presented a scene of beauty and peace but for the encampment of large bodies of troops along all the water courses.

"A rich prize, Barney," said Carlos at his side.

"Looks like they are more than ready for you, though, Carlos."

"Oh, yes. That could not be avoided, but it does not matter. It would be suicidal to meet them in the fields for they outnumber us many times. And besides the infantry that we can see, they will have at least as many mounted men, though they will be camped much farther away because they can move up so swiftly. But after all, it is the city we came for, and on this side it is vulnerable to our heavy naval guns. We will breach the walls and take the city in fighting in which their numbers can not be effective. Once inside, we can supply our troops from the water without opposition. Having Algiers, we can conquer all of Algeria at our leisure."

Joshua had secured a mooring about midway of the inner line of transports—a position that delighted him because it gave him a ringside seat for the fighting, which interested him far more than the money he would earn for Mr. Smith.

A day passed, and another day, while the ships swung idly at their anchors, the troops grumbled, and Carlos and his lieutenants grew increasingly impatient. The delay, Carlos said, was O'Reilly's fault entirely; the Spanish officers would have breached the walls before this.

On the following day at sunrise the boats came through the fleet, taking off officers of the rank of captain and higher, for a conference aboard the flagship. With his glass, Barney could see that her decks were packed with men, and several impassioned speeches were made. It seemed a strange way to start a battle.

In the afternoon when the officers returned to the ships, Sanchez came aboard with a tragic expression. To Jack and Joshua he gave no information, but Jack, loitering near and eavesdropping, overheard him tell his lieutenants that O'Reilly had ordered an immediate attack on the city by the naval guns, while Romana demanded that the troops be set ashore and the Moors vanquished in the sort of open fighting in which the perfectly-drilled Spaniards so clearly excelled.

Later, finding Joshua alone on the deck, Carlos confided to him with great indignation that O'Reilly had commanded Admiral de Castigon to bombard the city.

"That's the plan, isn't it?" Joshua asked.

"Oh, but Barney! For an upstart like that execrable O'Reilly to seek to command a man whose lineage was already ancient when Caesar conquered Gaul! Not even His Most Christian Majesty would presume to *command* a de Castigon! But there, you do not understand . . ."

"I perfectly understand." Barney's voice was bitter. "Your admiral will sink the whole expedition to save his sacred honor!"

Nevertheless, on the following morning, when Joshua opened his eyes as he lay upon the bare poop deck—where the whole afterguard slept in order to avoid the stifling heat of the ill-ventilated cabin—he saw that the warships were already forming a tight column and were heading straight for the city, as if to run themselves aground there. He called Carlos, and he and his two lieutenants leaped up and went to the rail.

By this time, every man aboard the *Sidney* was up. The soldiers stood massed on the main deck and forecastle, while the crew had taken to the rigging.

The flagship led the column, a leadsman in her forechains sounding as fast as he could throw the lead. When it seemed she must surely run herself aground, she turned hard to larboard, and when her guns bore upon the city, she fired her broadside. Instead of breaching the white-washed wall, however, her round shot raised great white geysers of salt water. Gasps and groans rose from the men of the *Sidney* for such incredibly bad marksmanship; and they turned their attention to the second ship in the column. Geysers of white water again!

Carlos and his lieutenants exchanged glances of utter incredulity, and the soldiers roared in derision.

The third ship did no better.

The *Sidney*'s people fell silent from sheer amazement,

but when the fourth ship repeated the performance exactly, Carlos exclaimed that O'Reilly was being put in his place.

He did not look happy about it, though, and as the childish farce continued, his expression became one of utter despair. He and his lieutenants stood alone at the rail as the hours passed, for neither Joshua nor Jack wanted to intrude.

Finally, at a word from Sanchez, the three officers turned and went down the companion ladder into the cabin. The African sun had already heated the deck planks over their heads until the pitch bubbled in the seams, and the little staterooms, being designed for keeping out the hostile sea rather than for letting in fresh air, would certainly, Joshua said, roast an ox. Right there they stayed, though, while the mockery continued, and continue it did until sundown. And not one round shot had struck the city the Armada had come to conquer.

"If O'Reilly hasn't had a stroke by this time," said Jack, "it's a miracle."

Immediately after the warships had ceased their empty thunders and returned to their moorings, a fleet of boats put out from the flagship, carrying written orders to all transports. Captain Barney received a requisition for the use of his longboat, and Sanchez, on deck once more, received an order to be prepared to embark his entire company at dawn.

"General Romana's plan has been adopted," he told Joshua. "We meet the enemy in the sort of fighting at which we so clearly excel." But there was no conviction in his voice. He stood at the poop-deck rail with Joshua and indicated the soldiers on the main deck, where they lay in little groups, laughing and talking, or gambling, or singing, or telling tall tales—their rage already forgotten.

"Tomorrow," he said, "they will go into battle, and before the sun has set many of them will be dead and many more will wish they were, for we are outnumbered three or four times and with all their valor and all the brilliance of our generals, our losses will be heavy."

"Too bad your admiral didn't go ahead and breach the walls."

"Unfortunately, my friend, that was the plan put forth by the abominable O'Reilly."

" 'Tis a pity, then, that O'Reilly didn't propose to fight it out in the open. Then your General Romana could have proposed the better plan."

"You are very understanding, Barney. But myself, I do not understand. No, myself I do not understand, for I should not permit you to say such things, Barney."

Joshua put his hand on the Spaniard's shoulder. "You are too loyal to your own class to say these things," he said, "and too honest to resent them when I say them. The truth is, your high command is ready to kill thousands of men and risk sinking your whole Armada rather than swallow even a small part of their pride."

"I must get my sleep, my friend. I am to make an early start."

"God go with you, Carlos." Joshua was deeply moved, for he greatly feared that tomorrow would see the end of his gallant friend. And Carlos, he knew, held the same thought.

CHAPTER SIXTEEN

THE BAY WAS LIKE GLASS THAT MOVED GENTLY IN SLOW undulations. The pennants of the warships hung limp. Light crept over the cloudless sky as night changed imperceptibly into dawn, and heat came ahead of the rising of the sun.

The thunder of one of the mighty cannon aboard the flagship boomed across the bay and rolled back from the hills of Algeria, and a flock of gulls rose from the water and with startled cries, fled seaward.

Carlos rose quickly from the deck where he had slept in nothing but his drawers after the stifling heat of the ill-ventilated cabin had driven him forth. His lieutenants bounded up after him, and Joshua stretched and yawned.

On the main deck a pock-marked, villainous-looking sergeant and several corporals were kicking the men awake.

The high, sweet notes of a bugle came clearly across the bay.

Jack and Joshua ate breakfast with the Spanish officers in the cabin but there was a feeling of urgency on all of them and they bolted their food and returned to the poop deck. On the main deck Joshua watched the soldiers wolfing their breakfast; then watched the distribution of arms.

Carlos, his face grave, shook hands with Jack, then with Joshua.

"God go with you, my friend," Joshua repeated. He exchanged ceremonious bows with the two lieutenants and wished them Godspeed, though he doubted that they understood a word of what he said. They would need God with them this day, though, if they were to see another dawn.

Carlos stood on the main deck at the foot of the companion ladder, watching his men over the rail and into the waiting boats. When all but a dozen of them had gone he sprang back up the ladder. He seized Joshua's shoulders in a hard grip. "Always remember, Barney," he said, "that I loved you like a brother!" Swiftly he kissed him on both cheeks and before Joshua could respond he was down the ladder, over the side and into the boat, and as it pulled away he never once glanced back.

Ashore, nothing was to be seen of the Moors. Their camps had disappeared. The earth seemed to have swallowed them.

As if at the pleasure of the mighty men of Spain, a breeze flawed the glassy surface of the water, lifted the pennants, and as it gained strength, flapped the sails of the warships. They were already formed in two columns almost a mile apart, heading toward the beach, and into the lane between them went the boats. Sails were sheeted home. The two columns moved ahead. They approached the shore. They turned aside, one to larboard, one to starboard, and as their guns bore upon the beach, they loosed their broadsides. This time their guns were aimed with skill and care, and round shot mowed down a field of wheat and a vineyard.

Beneath that hail of shot the boats ran aground and the soldiers waded ashore. Immediately the boats put off for more troops.

Jack and Joshua were trying to estimate the number in that first wave. There were just about six hundred boats, and as nearly as they could tell, there were about twelve men in each boat; say seven thousand men in round numbers. A third of their force. About a tenth of the enemy. And at that distance they looked like toy soldiers about an inch tall.

The offshore breeze held the *Sidney*'s head toward shore, and shrouds and other rigging cut across the view. This interference exasperated Joshua. He went to the forecastle, but still dissatisfied, he started aloft and kept going until he reached the main skysail yard. At such a distance from the battlefield, the added elevation was no help but at least he'd be alone and he didn't feel like talking to anybody. To his surprise, Jack had fearfully followed him in confident expectation of a much better view.

"Those monkeys wear uniforms fit for winter," said Jack. "I don't see how they endure it."

They sat on the spar, each with an arm about the mast, until it seemed about to cut their thighs in two. They shifted and squirmed. Joshua stood up on it, one arm around the slender tip of the mast, the other hand holding his spyglass to his eye. Jack squirmed about, his stomach queasy at the height, both his arms around the mast, until he sat astride with his feet on a rung of the little rope ladder just below them. He grumbled, but right there he stayed while the oarsmen pulled back to the transports, took the second wave of troops, and ferried them ashore.

Romana waved his sword and started up from the beach to the higher land. The cannonade ceased, lest the Spaniards walk right into it. Still no Moors had been sighted.

"Look up the hill, Jack!"

Jack looked. A body of cavalry was emerging from the lanes of an olive grove that was, perhaps, four or five miles beyond the Spaniards. It was not a strong force—about a thousand, Joshua estimated. At first he marvelled at the indifference of the Spaniards; then he realized that the Moors were hidden from them by the curve of the hill.

The bugle on the flagship sounded. The Spaniards looked about. The Moors appeared to them as they came over the brow of the hill. Lounging soldiers scrambled hastily to their feet. Officers waved their swords. Swiftly the soldiers closed their ranks.

"Romana agreed not to move a foot until the third wave gets ashore," Joshua said anxiously.

"That'll be quite a while," said Jack.

At a brisk trot the Moors had advanced to within a quarter of a mile of the Spaniards. There, they slowed down, came on a little further, and halted completely. There was an appearance of confusion among the Moorish cavalry.

"I think they're just a bit of cheese to bait a rattrap."

"I think so myself. Romana'll hardly be taken in, though." But Jack sounded uncertain.

"He'd hardly be taken in if O'Reilly hadn't warned him. He might get taken in now just to prove how independent he is of that Irishman."

The confusion among the Moors seemed to be increasing. Some advanced, then retreated, while others came through the first lot, advanced a bit further, and then they, also, retreated. Each advance was a bit nearer to the motionless Spaniards. Finally a dozen of them loosed a ragged volley from their long carabines, then bolted back and lost themselves among their fellows. The Spaniards ignored them. They advanced still nearer, and a score of them took careful aim and fired. One of the Spanish officers, standing well in advance of the troops, sagged slowly out of sight beyond his men.

A sword flashed. There was motion in the ranks of the Spaniards and a long line of black puffs leaped from their muskets. A few of the Moors retreated a short distance but none fell.

"I have heard," said Jack, "that their carabines outrange the Spanish muskets."

"They must have the range down pretty fine, then."

Again the Moors advanced. Again a score of them fired.

Another officer dropped from sight.

Firing now became general. The Spaniards were loading and firing steadily, at every Moorish advance. A horse reared, pawed the air, and raced straight at the Spanish ranks. His rider slid to the ground and tumbled over and over, scrambled to his feet and was immediately brought down by Spanish fire.

The next Moorish volley came from a hundred pieces and got a dozen Spaniards. A few, wounded, sat or lay behind their line while their comrades bandaged them; then started a slow, painful journey to the rear; others were laid out on the grass, to writhe or to lie still under the fierce African sun.

"Think Romana'll wait for that next wave?" Joshua asked anxiously, eyeing the laboring boats. They had not yet reached the transports and the oarsmen had not paused for food or drink.

"I doubt it, Josh."

The words were hardly spoken when the whole Spanish line began to deploy and then to move forward.

From the flagship came the sound of a bugle blowing the retreat. If Romana heard it, he gave no sign. On he went, his sword flashing high over his head at every stride, and his men went after him, pausing at regular intervals to fire.

The bugle repeated the retreat. Its notes rose piercingly on the heavy air, cracked, and started again. Ahead of the Spaniards the Moors fired and wheeled and fired again. Here one Spaniard, there two or three, dropped back, to lie still, or to writhe, or to sit and bandage himself and to start once more the slow, painful journey under that blistering sun.

The slow advance continued. The bugle finally fell silent.

"O'Reilly'll have a stroke," said Barney.

"Aye."

A short distance from the left flank of the advancing Spaniards there was a large olive grove, and now, as the invading line passed it, a small band of Moorish infantry —perhaps a hundred men—emerged from it, took careful aim, and enfiladed the Spaniards. A dozen of them fell.

Immediately a detachment of Spaniards split off from the main body and went after the Moors, who had fired once and fled. The grove swallowed up pursued and pursuers, and neither Barney nor Jack saw them again.

Now the pattern of the battle was horribly clear and it

was exactly what O'Reilly had warned against. Over the immense field—over the rolling hills and into little valleys, in pastures and groves and vineyards—Moors and Spaniards milled in what appeared from the masthead to be a hopeless confusion. The battle spread out over miles of territory and continued to spread. Under the broiling sun, in their heavy uniforms and loaded with powder and lead, the Spaniards marched and countermarched, pursued and were pursued.

In groves and vineyards innumerable small forts were cleverly concealed. Bands of cavalry, repeating the tactics of that first detachment, swirled in front of the Spaniards, retreated, and led them under the guns of the forts; then, as soon as the Spanish pieces had been fired, the Moors rode into them at full gallop, slashing with their keen, curved blades. The slaughter was bad and getting worse while confusion among the Spanish ranks increased.

Surely those sixteen thousand men would be wiped out before the third wave could be set ashore.

Then, almost in a moment, the appearance of the battle changed. After it was all over, Joshua and Jack learned the explanation; but at the moment it was like the trick of a magician. Romana fell with three slugs in his chest and belly, and he had hardly hit the ground when his second in command sounded a bugle. Aboard the *Sidney* that call could not be heard but it could be seen, and its effect was amazing. "To me! To me!" No pantomime could have been clearer.

Again and again it must have sounded, and the little toy soldiers responded with frantic zeal, for to them it was a reprieve from what they must have seen clearly meant swift destruction.

Around that new commander a huge, hollow figure began to take shape. Sometimes, as it moved, and grew, it was almost square; sometimes, a rough circle or some odd shape, according to the terrain; but ever it grew as more of the small, scattered bands coalesced with it. In its center went the walking wounded, with a few whole men to help along those who could not quite walk alone; and every cavalry detachment that sought to draw it into ambush was met by a murderous volley but nothing more.

Now that huge, hollow figure, having gathered up all scattered bands, began a slow, deliberate movement back toward the beach-head, and the watchers aboard the *Sidney*, drawing long breaths of relief, turned their fascinated gaze from the battle to the boats.

Some of them were already arriving at the transports. Soldiers were tumbling into them in frantic haste. They handed down picks and shovels as well as arms, and each boat, as it was loaded, set off directly for the beach-head without waiting to move in formation. The oarsmen were straining at their oars but the deep-laden boats seemed to Barney to creep like snails.

"Sir," said Mr. Barnes, "I brung you summat to eat and drink."

Looking down, Joshua saw his entire crew in the rigging. Mr. Barnes was on the little rope ladder to which Carlos had clung. He reached down gratefully for the bundle and the jug that Mr. Barnes passed up to him.

"Sir," said Mr. Barnes, "I made certain they was all done for."

"Aye, and a lot of 'em are done for." And Carlos might be one of those; it was maddening to be unable to tell.

For the last hour or so, Joshua now realized, the Spanish

fire had been gradually slackening. Evidently their ammunition was running out.

Clouds of cavalry separated them from their beach-head, and the Moorish strategy was terrifyingly clear. Simply, it was to keep the invaders from contact with reinforcements until their ammunition was fully exhausted.

The Spaniards were moving more rapidly toward their beach-head, where the first boats were arriving and soldiers were splashing ashore. The warships opened fire again, shooting over the heads of the men. The round shot rolled and bounded to meet the cavalry, which now was being crowded toward the beach by the steady advance of the Spaniards. A ball smashed a horse and rider. A few more horses went down. With a volley that must have taken very nearly the last of their ammunition, the Spaniards pressed more swiftly toward the beach, and the cavalry, dreading those bounding cannon balls, cleared out of that space.

The cannonade ceased, and about two hundred of the new arrivals—all that had come ashore so far—set out at the double to join their comrades. To Joshua's spyglass, every one of them appeared bowed down under a staggering load of *cartouches,* and at the joyful reunion the fresh ammunition was passed swiftly about the circle.

The cavalry continued to press attacks from three sides, but now the Spaniards no longer had to conserve ammunition; all of them were firing; and the Moorish charges were more costly.

As more boats arrived and the soldiers ran up to the high ground, instead of joining in the battle they fell upon a prepared line with pick and shovel; and as the numbers of the picks and shovels increased, a mile-long trench grew swiftly.

The battle had raged to within a little over a mile of the trench, and there the invaders, after receiving still more ammunition, made a stand. They even began a slow return toward the hills, as if determined to wipe out all the Moors without recourse to fortifications of even the simplest sort. If that was the plan, however, it was more than at least one exhausted soldier, caught in the center of Barney's lens, could endure; for suddenly he flung down his musket and fled toward the beach. After him went another, then three more, and in a moment a dozen were in full flight and while Barney gazed in horror, that magnificent formation began dissolving like morning mist under the rising sun.

Frantically the officers ran among the men, striving to turn them—even cutting some down with their swords— but every man on the field was suddenly certain that if he tarried a moment he would be left entirely alone to face the hordes of savage Moors. One moment they were an army, magnificent and deadly; the next moment they were a frenzied mob. To Joshua, it was still so sudden he could scarcely believe the clear evidence of his own eyes.

Now horror was piled on horror. The Moorish cavalry entered upon an orgy of slaughter that must have exceeded their fondest dreams, for in that melee the guns of the warships were helpless to select friend from foe, and the cavalry dashed, slashing, through that fleeing mob; wheeled, and dashed again.

For a time it seemed that not a man would survive; yet many did; and in terror, leaped the growing mile-long pile of earth that separated them from the shelter of the trench.

The officer in command there, on seeing the start of the flight, had ordered his men to drop picks and shovels and seize arms; and as the frenzied fugitives began leaping into the trench he opened fire at close range on the per- suing cavalry. The astonished Moors, balked of the final massacre, fled, leaving many dead and wounded; but in their retreat they worked a bloody revenge on those Spanish wounded who littered the path of the flight.

Now the entire Spanish force was ashore, and the oarsmen were set to ferrying supplies to them. By dark they had transported a mountain of food and ammunition, and even a few small cannon. However, the soldiers who had endured that day's fighting wanted no more of it, and in small groups at first, then in larger numbers, they turned to seizing the boats as fast as they were unloaded, and forcing the oarsmen to row them to the transports.

Joshua's first intimation of this phase of the flight came well after dark, when he heard the *thunk* of oars on thole pins, and then a few groans. Hurrying to the rail, he saw the boats, mere blobs of denser black against the black water. They came alongside and he flung out the rope ladders. Perhaps Carlos, badly wounded, would be among them. Or he might get word of him. Many of those who came over the side wore bloody bandages, but half of them were unhurt.

Jack tried to talk to them, but some appeared stunned or dazed, some surly, and some ashamed, and he got little out of them. He asked about Captain Sanchez, and got nothing.

As more boats came by, Joshua stood at the rail with

Jack, who called to know if Captain Sanchez was aboard them; and when he was answered in the negative, he sent them on to other transports.

The night wore on. The boats thinned and, about dawn, they ceased; and Joshua did not then or ever learn what his friend's fate had been.

By that time, the Moors were about again, reconnoitering the trench. They descended upon the heaped-up supplies like immense swarms of vultures on carrion and in an amazingly short time they carried all of it away. Then they turned to cleaning up the battle field, lest that July sun breed a pestilence from the thousands of corpses.

The ships swung idly at their anchors.

A dozen boats put out from the warships and made for the nearest transports, and grim-faced men boarded ship after ship, one man to a ship. The supplies that had been taken off the night before had scarcely dented the immense stores still in the holds, and these visitors commandeered crews and went to searching the cargoes. The man who had boarded the *Sidney* was in a vile temper, and when asked what he was hunting for, snapped that it was nobody's business. Later, Mr. Barnes reported that under his direction a dozen soldiers had laboriously moved enough of the cargo for every piece of it to be examined; but the man left empty-handed.

After a full week of searching the entire fleet, the Armada catted its anchors and sailed for Cartagena. As Barney brought the *Sidney* onto her course, another transport sailed close alongside, and her captain called across the narrow strip of water.

"Find anything aboard of you, Captain?"

"Not a thing. Aboard of you?"

"Know what they was lookin' for?"

"No, but I have a guess."

"Gunpowder?"

"That's mine."

"I'll lay my ship to your longboat you're right. If they'd had any more gunpowder, wouldn't they of took their revenge on that town?"

"Most certainly."

"I'll lay you there's a warehouse somewhere back in Spain that's crammed to the eaves with about ten thousand barrels of powder that was meant for this Armada and the monkeys come off an' forgot it!"

CHAPTER SEVENTEEN

RAIN PELTED DOWN. THE SAILS SCOOPED BUCKETS OF IT FROM the lazy breeze and dumped it in extra torrents on the deck. Captain Barney, having grown prodigiously in the last year, almost filled out the glistening oilskins that Captain Drysdale had once worn, but his crew disdained their clumsy tarred canvas suits and went about bare to the waist, their breeches hacked off above the knee and the soles of their feet as black and tough as dogs' feet.

On all sides, dim ghosts of ships loomed through the rain, sailed with the *Sidney*, paced her, kept their distance.

A few sullen Spaniards, indifferent to the warm rain, stood or sat against the weather rail, while one, very seasick, hung over the lee rail; but most of the two-hundred-odd soldiers the *Sidney* carried had sought shelter in the cargo hold where removal of supplies had left a little space.

Joshua had deputized Jack to deal with them, since he spoke the language; but that arrangement wasn't working well because the Spaniards were in a foul temper and were showing their feeling for the British more freely than they would otherwise have done. They were, Jack reported, angry and bewildered. Their tolerance for the fantastic personal pride of their grandees was beyond the comprehension of anybody but another Spaniard; but even that tolerance had been outraged by the betrayal of the Armada, and Jack thought that all they would need to start bloodshed, if they could just find a scapegoat, would be an inflammatory leader. Joshua, in consequence, was apprehensive about his charter fee, for if he couldn't collect that, he would have wasted much time and have run up expenses that Mr. Smith would hold against him. Moreover, he was desperately anxious to be among the first to call for cargoes in the overstocked trading ports of the coast; he was certain that bargains awaited those first buyers. The ships that he could dimly see through the rain were a very small fraction of the fleet that was hurrying back to Cartagena, and other captains were doubtless just as anxious about those generous charter fees and trade bargains.

On top of this anxiety came another thought to plague him. The latest news he'd had from the Colonies, where war with England had been threatened, must now be at least five months old; no knowing what might have happened in that time. The British warships might be seizing American merchant ships wherever they could find them. Well, there was nothing he could do about that, and he pushed the thought from him in order to concentrate on a problem he could do something about. No question about it; he simply had to get into Cartagena ahead of these other transports. He squinted into the rain. Were the clouds thinning a little in the southwest? He thought so.

"Mr. Barnes!" he called, "I'll have the staysails, if you please, Mr. Barnes! All hands! Drive her, Mr. Barnes! Drive her!"

"Aye, aye, sir!" Mr. Barnes replied with alacrity, called

all hands, and sent them scurrying about the setting of the staysails.

The ghost ships were looming clearer as the rain slacked, and more ships were coming into view. Gradually the rain ceased; the clouds thinned. The ragged overcast became patched with blue and the patches grew and ran together. Ships, ships; ships were everywhere, as far as the eye could see!

Joshua had been eager for a ringside anchorage from which to view the fighting ashore, and had got it; now he was paying for it in the number of transports still ahead of him. With a fresh breeze he could cross from Algiers to Cartagena in three days or even in two, but yesterday and today there had been barely enough breeze for steerage way and at this rate it might take him ten days or two weeks. Well, the time didn't matter; the point was, he must gain on those vessels that had got out of the Bay of Algiers ahead of him. He drew an imaginary line to larboard and to starboard, at right angles to his course, and tried to count the ships that were ahead of that line. About a third of the entire fleet, he estimated. He studied his sagging canvas again. He went down onto the main deck and walked forward along the weather rail, head far back, eyes anxiously scanning the mountains of still-dripping canvas over his head. He directed the trimming of a sail here and a sail there, but if there was space to set as much as another pocket handkerchief, he couldn't find it. He studied the sky, now almost clear, and the wind. The breeze was freshening. Well, that was hopeful. That might give him an advantage, for the *Sidney* was a stout ship in a blow; he'd pit her against the best. And he'd dare another master to match him carrying sail!

As the breeze freshened, seasick soldiers started crawling out of the hold to hang over the rail. Soon, now that the rain had ceased, his whole deck would be choked with them, and that would be no advantage for handling sail.

By noon the breeze was blowing half a gale from the southwest, and the following seas smacked the *Sidney*'s larboard quarter with a force that gave the ship a corkscrew motion and Mr. Barnes had to set another man to help hold the bucking wheel. Half the soldiers were violently seasick over both the rails or all over the deck, and the disgusted sailors kept the big chain pump and the leather hose busy sluicing down.

Some of the ships ahead had already shortened sail and the *Sidney* was gaining briskly on most of them. The warships, that had so arrogantly herded the transports on the outward voyage, were now scattered among the fleet, some far astern, some apparently making for other ports. Joshua wondered briefly if those haughty grandees who had scuttled the expedition to save their own inordinate pride were pleased with themselves, but that was no problem of his and he shrugged it off.

It was evident that every transport was steering her own course, for a few of them were veering a degree or two to larboard, others a little to starboard, of the *Sidney*. The fastest ship in the fleet could be the last one to port if her master was just a few degrees out in his calculations, and Joshua set himself to concentrate on his navigation. He was pitted now against much older and more experienced seamen. How would he show up in such company? Pride in his craft was deeply involved; but beyond that, the whole success or failure of the entire voyage might be decided by the accuracy with which he plotted a course for the Bay of Cartagena. For the harbor facilities of the town could scarcely handle the unloading of more than eight or ten vessels at one time, if that many, so unless he could be among the first, he would have to lie to his anchor for weeks while more fortunate vessels were unloaded.

Dawn saw more ships dropped astern, and all that day Joshua, Jack and the crew watched as the hard-driven *Sidney* overhauled ship after ship. Whatever Captain Barney wanted, he wanted with an intensity that was contagious; and the sailors pushed their way among the sullen soldiers, sweated at the lines, raced aloft, and cheered like school boys at every transport they overtook and passed.

It was on the sixth day out of the Bay of Algiers that the racing *Sidney* swept past the fortified island and the grim, ancient forts that guarded the entrance to the Bay of Cartagena, and the immense bowl of barren, red and yellow crags that surrounded the magnificent harbor opened out before them. Only five of the transports were ahead of her, but dozens were crowding close on her heels and Joshua kept every stitch of canvas drawing until he was within half a mile of the city's piers. By that time, the first of the transports had docked and two more were being warped into their berths, soldiers had been sighted on the decks, and the water front swarmed with people. It looked as if every man, woman and child had turned out to welcome their victorious heroes.

Joshua and Jack watched anxiously as the first of the ships discharged her quota of sullen soldiers. Under Mr. Barnes's command, the *Sidney's* sails were flapping and being furled, and the ship was losing headway; her crew was struggling about among the press of soldiers on the deck, but Joshua ignored all of that as he watched the crowd about the soldiers who had already gone ashore.

For a while the cheering continued unabated. Maybe, Joshua thought, they aren't going to tell about their defeat. Or maybe they just can't make themselves heard. Gradually, though, the nature of the crowd's voice changed. It was a subtle change, a slight lull in total volume and a slight alteration in tone; but as the *Sidney* drew alongside a pier, the change was unmistakable. Word was passing from lip to lip through the crowd as the sorry tale spread. Two other transports began discharging soldiers; the news spread more swiftly. Here and there an angry shout rose against the solid volume of sound; the murmur grew and swelled as hundreds of angry voices became a few thousand; and an ominous roar echoed between the bare hills.

People swarmed alongside the *Sidney;* soldiers went over her rail, carefully handed down their badly wounded and those few who had died on the voyage. The crowd stood and watched. The royal welcome had turned sour, but as yet the mood of the people seemed to be a sort of angry dismay.

An officer leaped onto a bollard and started to harangue the crowd.

"He's blaming O'Reilly," Jack translated. "Not entirely, though," he added a little later. "He's giving 'em some pretty plain facts. He's mighty bitter against the Spanish generals."

The crowd, which had been silent while he talked, burst into another, fiercer roar. The soldiers pushed through toward the head of the pier and the streets of the town, and the people went with them. The pier was abandoned. Other ships docked, until every possible berth was taken and all others had to wait at anchor. Soldiers disembarked on deserted piers, for the crowd had turned its collective back on them; but the ominous roar continued throughout the afternoon while the people milled about in the streets.

Jack went ashore to see what he could learn; an hour later he was back aboard looking very thoughtful. "A few of the officers are working the people up against their own generals," he said. "But the generals won't come in here, and these people want blood. They just might take their rage out on any scapegoat they can find. By tonight, when they're full of wine, there's no telling. They might even turn on the transports. You'll be a lot safer, Josh, if you'll tow out a mile or so and drop your mud hook."

"Maybe; but there isn't dock space for a tenth of the fleet. If I give up the berth here, I might be just about the last ship to get unloaded. I'll lay you anything you like there isn't half enough gold in this town to pay the charter fees of all these ships; and the first one out of here will have the pick of all the stocks of goods that have been piling up in the warehouses at the other ports. No, sir, Jack. Right here I stay, barring an attack in force, until I'm unloaded and paid off.

"Mr. Barnes!"

"Aye, aye, sir."

"Mr. Barnes, I'm going ashore. I don't want any of these monkeys coming aboard. Issue marlinespikes to the crew, but keep 'em out of sight. Likely you won't be bothered at all, but if any of the natives do come down the pier, just keep an eye on 'em and keep 'em off; but don't antagonize 'em if you don't have to."

"Aye, aye, sir."

"And put the longboat alongside with a towing cable bent on. If any of the transports are attacked, cast off and tow out a safe distance. I'm leaving her in your hands, Mr. Barnes."

"Aye, aye, sir! That I will, sir!"

"Come along, then, Jack. Let's go see if we can find anybody that can speak English."

"You won't get any action today, Josh."

"I don't expect it. I just want to do a little reconnoitering to see if I can get in ahead of these other captains. Then, when things quiet down, I'll know where to start."

"A smart idea, I expect," said Jack, and he followed Joshua over the side.

Walking along the pier, Jack suggested that they try the government offices anyway. "Prob'ly won't be a soul in 'em, but can you fancy finding anybody in that mob?"

"That mob" was a milling crowd that occupied the entire water front and overflowed a little onto the shore end of every pier; and the force of Jack's remark was only too evident. Men and women were swirling about in aimless confusion, rushing from one little group to another, shouting and gesticulating in a manner to suggest to a cooler temperament that they were on the point of tearing each other to bloody shreds. Actually, they were agreeing wholeheartedly on the blackhearted manner of their betrayal; and they were demanding the blood of General O'Reilly and of some of the Spanish generals.

"Those generals aren't coming in here," Jack bawled at Joshua's ear, "but this mob is thirsty for blood. They'll be looking for a scapegoat, most likely, and that will be the nearest Englishman or any vessel flying the British flag."

Joshua shouldered his way into the seething crowd, and Jack followed close. He hoped to find the same official with whom he had arranged the terms of the charter, and he headed straight for the building in which that transaction had been conducted. They found the street door standing open, and they entered the wide, dimly-lighted hall. Doors stood open on both sides, but the only sounds came from the street. They looked into every office. Deserted—completely deserted. Every clerk, every functionary from highest to lowest was in the street. They returned to the front of the building and entered an office on their right, where they stood at a window and tried to see through a pane of glass that certainly had not been washed for years and probably not since the building had been erected.

"Sun's low," Joshua said. "Don't you think somebody'll come back here to lock up for the night?"

"Maybe they don't lock up at night."

"Seems like they would, at least if there's money enough in here to pay my charter fee. Can't find anybody out there, though. We might as well wait."

Twilight filled the room, but their patience paid off at last, for a man entered. He paused in the doorway and peered sharply at them in the dim light. They bowed deeply, and he bowed also. He looked, Joshua thought, responsible; and when he spoke he had an air of birth and breeding, and of authority.

Jack conversed with him briefly when, to his surprise, Joshua heard him say, "I speak English." Excellent Eng-

221

lish, too. But by that time, he had sensed that the Spaniard was in the grip of strong emotion, and suddenly he felt very much out of place, like a peddler trying to sell his wares at a funeral. Perhaps he had made a bad blunder in trying to urge his own affairs on a Spaniard on the very day of such a disaster. He should have allowed a decent interval for mourning. But Jack was already introducing the man as Colonel Spatello, and the colonel asked Captain Barney his pleasure. He still spoke with the courtly grace of a Spanish gentleman, but in the direct contact Joshua felt much more forcibly the emotion that almost overpowered him.

"Señor Colonel," Joshua said diffidently, hoping he could emulate the manner and the form of address that he had liked in Carlos, "if it is not too great a presumption, my friend and I wish merely, at this time, to express our great sympathy for the disaster that General O'Reilly has brought upon Spanish arms. We witnessed the hero- ism of your men."

The Colonel bowed deeply. "I thank you, Captain," he said with evident appreciation. "You are gentlemen of rare sensibility. But you do have business to transact with me?"

"At a more appropriate time, Señor Colonel. Today we wish only to express our very great sympathy."

"At a more appropriate time, then, it will be my very great pleasure to serve you, Captain. If you will call upon me here, in midmorning, the day after tomorrow, all will be as you wish."

"I thank you, Señor Colonel. It shall be as you suggest. Good night, Señor Colonel."

"Go with God, Captain."

Jack and Joshua exchanged ceremonious bows with the Colonel, and withdrew. On the steps outside the street door, they paused before plunging back into the crowd. Jack regarded Joshua with a thoughtful smile. "Burn me, Josh," he said, "I knew you were a good seaman, but I didn't know you were a first-rate diplomat, too. You learn fast, my friend."

"It hit me all of sudden, Jack. He looked so unhappy."

"A mighty lucky hit." And they plunged once more into the swirling crowd.

All that night the town was in an uproar. Joshua ordered a vigilant lookout from the masthead for the first sign of trouble on any of the transports, and himself came on deck several times during the night, prepared on a moment's notice to cast off and tow out to safety; but the rioters did not molest the transports. He suspected, from the sounds that reached him, that there were some savage fights in streets and *cantinas*, but if so, they were strictly personal affairs, for there was no sign of any concerted action. The next day passed quietly as far as the *Sidney* and her people were concerned, though the town was still demoralized, and at sunrise on the following day a crew of stevedores arrived and started unloading the *Sidney*. About ten thirty, Captain Barney presented himself at the office of Colonel Spatello. He was received with courtly grace. He complimented the colonel on such promptness in unloading. He endured with patience while impersonal trivialities were discussed, as convention demanded, but eventually the colonel himself brought the conversation around to business.

"And now, Captain," he said, "you desire to collect your charter fee. You have your contract with you?"

Joshua handed it over. The colonel, with the aid of a calendar, counted the days, allowed three more for unloading, and computed the amount of the fee. He took a huge key from a drawer in his desk. It was of brass, at least a foot long, and designed to operate the works of a truly massive lock, for the bits were as thick as Joshua's first finger, the shank was as thick as his wrist, and the terminal was broader that the palm of his hand, and of a rich and beautiful design. With it the colonel opened a very massive, iron-studded door and from the strong room he brought a leather bag that he carried with evident effort. When he set it on his desk, Joshua heard the dull clunk of coins, and from it the colonel brought forth gold pieces and counted out the fee. The amount was not quite the largest sum Joshua had ever handled at one time, but it was enough nevertheless to produce a lordly feeling of great opulence. He signed a receipt, and the transaction was closed.

"And now, Captain," the colonel said, "before you sail I hope you and your friend will do me the honor to dine with me and tell me all about the battle that you witnessed. Will tomorrow evening be agreeable?"

"Most agreeable, Excellency. I will be delighted."

The colonel laughed. "For this unmerited promotion to the exalted rank of Excellency, my thanks, Captain," he said. "I will look forward with pleasure to the honor of receiving you at seven o'clock. Until then, go with God, Captain."

The city was still demoralized all that day, and the *Sidney* was the only transport that was being unloaded. Joshua was besieged by captains who wanted to know how he did it.

"Diplomacy," said Jack, at his side.

"Colonel Spatello," said Joshua.

But Colonel Spatello, it seemed, could not be found, and Joshua was torn in two directions. His natural impulse was to help the other captains as much as he could; but if the colonel was avoiding them for reasons of his own, then it might be a serious breach of his hospitality to tell them that he was dining with him, or to give them directions for finding his home. Surely they could dig up that much information for themselves. And after all, Joshua did not know where the stevedores came from. The colonel had spoken; they had appeared and gone to work. No doubt, by the time the *Sidney* was unloaded and away, the city would have settled down to normal again and all the stevedores would be ready to return to work. After all, this arrangement was barely enough to give Joshua the lead he wanted on other captains in his search for return cargo. By late afternoon, he and Jack stood alone once more on the quarter-deck, and Jack had an opportunity to say that he had arranged for passage directly to Gibraltar with a British vessel that would be sailing that way long before the *Sidney* would; he had been away long enough and should be reporting back there to carry his end of the business. It was the sensible thing to do and Joshua could not object; but he knew that he would miss his friend. For a lad who loved people as Joshua did, his was a lonely job.

They were discussing this matter when still another visitor came aboard—a skipper with a cold gray eye and a businesslike manner who immediately announced that he had a vastly different proposition from all those importunate captains who wanted something for nothing.

"I," he said, "offer you a swap that you can't afford to miss."

"What can you offer me?"

"News, Barney. News straight from home. And in return, I want your help here so's I can swap my cargo of wheat and barrel staves for goods of this port."

"You're right from home?"

"That's right, Barney. I wasn't in this cockeyed Armada. I'm straight from home. They tell me you have got a way of gettin' what you want out of these monkeys, an' I can't get along with 'em at all. But I've got news'll be worth a handsome profit on your return cargo. Speak a good word for me with Spatello, get me in to see him, an' the news is yours."

Joshua looked up and around at the utterly barren ramparts of treeless, grassless rock that towered above the city and the bay. "What can Cartagena produce that you can use?" he asked. "Rock for ballast?"

Captain Clinton smiled a thin little smile. "That's my worry. You help me to make my swap; I'll give you what'll be worth more to you than what I get."

Joshua was puzzled. He greatly desired news—any news —from home, for he had been away many months; but Captain Clinton seemed to think it would have commercial value. He was clearly in earnest, too, and he was a man who inspired confidence. "I've got to lay in a certain cargo at a certain port," Joshua told him. "It's all written in my orders. I have no discretion. Then I'm for home. I don't see how any news you have can change my plans or be worth a profit on my cargo."

"What have you got to lose? Think it over if you want to, but don't be too long about it."

The threats of war with England had never been very far from Joshua's mind since before he had left Gibraltar, and they occurred to him now. "War with England!" he exclaimed.

"And you got Gibraltar to pass!" said Captain Clinton. "So you know. How come you're fiddlin' away your time here, then?"

"I didn't *know*. I only heard it was a possibility before I left the Rock. I hoped it would never happen."

"It's happened," and Captain Clinton told him about the fighting around Boston. "You picked your side?" he asked.

"I'll go with Maryland."

"All right, then. Maryland's in it. They're all in it. All thirteen of 'em. So I'll put it to you like this. We need powder an' lead worst of anything. That's what I want. There ought to be plenty of it in these government warehouses, seems as though. Can you help me get it?"

"If it's to be used against the British, they'll most likely give it to you. I'm dining with Colonel Spatello tonight. I'll speak to him about it. Maybe I can lay in a bit of it myself, on top of my other cargo."

"You could. But be all set to run a British blockade if you do, though. If they stop you anywhere and find contraband on you, bingo, they'll nab your ship and slap you into their navy."

"How about you?"

"I own my ship, an' runnin' a British blockade in New England waters is my trade. I been free-tradin' around there for years. There's tricks to learn, though, an' peace time is the time to learn 'em. You got a mighty fine ship here."

"I see. Well, anyway, I'll do all I can for you."

"You still aim to take time for a cargo?"

"Why not? If they nab me, they'll nab me with a cargo or without, won't they? And with or without contraband, for that matter."

"They warn't nabbin' Americans when I come past the Rock. They can start any day. They're bound to, sooner or later."

"Well, I'm not going back without a cargo, but I prob'ly won't take any contraband. I reckon I owe that much to my owner. See me tomorrow and I'll tell you what Colonel Spatello says."

CHAPTER EIGHTEEN

ON A SWELTERING DAY LATE IN AUGUST A LAZY BREEZE wafted the *Sidney* into the harbor of Alicante. It was her second visit to that port since she had left the cringing governor at Nice, and now, as on the former visit, the bay was bare of ships.

The Spanish breeze, with a true Spanish indolence that was very different from the prompt energy Barney had met in Cartagena, was taking no account of his impatience. He sought a spot of shade on the main deck, and tried to train his soul to patience while he watched his sails pucker and droop, pucker and droop, in the listless air. He stood with his arms spread on the rail at his back, sweat streaming down his face and his whole body. He thought of Jack, and missed him. A captain's was a lonely job. He thought of Pam. In his mind's eye he saw the delighted smile with which she would welcome him if he dared stop off at Gibraltar, and he wondered a little about his own feeling. He thought of the Maryland girls he had met from time to time at home between voyages. They were vague shadows in his memory. Not one of them had ever meant anything to him; they were just friends of his sisters and more or less in the way, but

Pam was warm and vivid and for a moment at parting her lips had been sweet fire. I couldn't do better, he thought. Maybe, when we get this war settled, if I don't find anybody I like better in the meantime . . . If she still loves me. Women are said to be mighty fickle. Oh, well, plenty of time for that.

Moving so deliberately on that indolent Spanish air that she left scarcely a ripple in her wake, the ship advanced to the city piers and was warped to a berth, and Barney went to call upon Mr. Smith's agent, a Mr. Harrison. He proved to be a tall, thin man, sandy-haired, with his scalp starting to show through on top.

If the Englishman had heard of the war between his own country and the Colonies, it did not show in his cordial greeting. Oh, yes, he had heard of the adventure with that thieving governor at Nice. Barney's fame had gone all up and down the coast. Those Vespucci brothers were notorious. "Very creditable, sir. Very creditable indeed. But tell me about the affair of Algiers. It did come off, I suppose? And were you in it? Yes, I'll wager you were as close to the fighting as you could get and remain afloat! Do tell me about it, sir!"

"It did," said Barney with a laugh, "and I was," and he spent an hour in a description of the fiasco. Finally, though, even that subject was exhausted, and they got around to a discussion of business.

"I have buckets of gold, sir," Barney said. "I am prepared to lay in a high-priced cargo. Silks, wines, and olive oil are my orders. How is the market?"

"All yours, Captain. All yours. We have had so little trade since the Spaniards started chartering ships for their Armada that the warehouses are bulging and the merchants are eager to sell. I can drive some very sharp bargains for you."

Barney found the market as Mr. Harrison had described it, and under his guidance he saw the best of the stocks. Mr. Harrison steered him clear of exporters' tricks, and he laid in a cargo that promised huge profits at home. And in those profits, as captain, Barney would have a share. Enough, he thought with amusement, to set up housekeeping—when he should feel like it.

That is, he amended, he would have a share in it if the British didn't nab him on the way home. And all that the British warships had to do in order to capture him or any of the American vessels then in the Mediterranean was to wait and pick them up, like picking apples off a tree, as they sought to pass the Rock. It was as simple as that.

Given a stormy night, though, a fast vessel, smartly handled, just might be able to slip past those watchful British warships. Barney was doing two things at once. Stowing cargo was Mr. Barnes' responsibility, but he was new and untrained in that capacity, and if any of those casks of wine or olive oil should work loose in a heavy sea and go crashing about among the rest of the cargo, great damage could be done. Ships had even been known to sink because of a shifted cargo. So Barney was below in the stifling hold, giving Mr. Barnes a word of advice as needed. At the same time, he was trying to weigh the possibilities of evading the squadron of British warships at Gibraltar, but that was a tough problem because it was compounded of so many unknowns. He didn't even know for a fact that it was necessary to evade them; he merely had to assume that it was.

So, if he could wait out the fine weather in a friendly Spanish port very near Gibraltar, then on a night of wind and rain he might be able to get clear out into the Atlantic before dawn; but was there such a port, deep enough for the *Sidney?* Cartagena was two hundred miles from Gibraltar. Even Malaga was seventy miles away; much too far. Estepona was about twenty-five miles. It might do, but Barney knew nothing about its harbor, and on that point Mr. Harrison had not been able to help him. The Spanish merchants had assured him that he would find ample water there, but he was still doubtful; they might be speaking more from national pride than from exact knowledge. He decided to put into Malaga and inquire; the port authorities there would know. One way or another, though, he felt sure he could use Estepona. He didn't think the British would patrol that part of the coast. They had no reason to. But if they did, and if he could not enter the harbor, a large ship like the *Sidney* would excite much less curiosity in the mind of a British naval commander if he saw her standing just off a shallow Spanish port than the same ship would excite if she were seen at anchor off a barren coast. So with his cargo securely stowed and his hatches battened down, he sailed out of Alicante Bay and seventeen days later he dropped his anchor in deep water in the harbor of Estepona.

Now was the time to pray for stormy weather, for when the sun sank behind the western hills there was not a cloud in the sky. No telling how long he would have to wait.

As it turned out, he spent only a week there; and it was just as well, too, for the enforced idleness was demoralizing to a crew that had been too long from home and was impatient to return. They grumbled; they might have to swing to their anchor in that forlorn hole for a month, or even for two months. Barney could not blame them, for he was the most impatient man aboard—though that was something he had to conceal, for if the crew saw his impatience they would only be confirmed and increased in their own.

The eighth day dawned hopefully, however, for the sky was overcast and fitful gusts of wind eddied down from the hills and whipped up spiteful little whitecaps in the sheltered harbor. By midmorning it was blowing half a gale and rain swept the bay in erratic sheets that came and went, alternately revealing and concealing the surrounding hills. If it kept on like that all night, it would be as good as a man could want, but Barney would have been much better pleased if it had started in the afternoon; it was too likely to blow over by nightfall. But the weather was always a seaman's gamble. If the storm held until early afternoon, he'd have to chance it. His only problem then would be the current in the Gut.

That same current had saved him once, now so many eventful months ago, when it had swept his foundering ship and exhausted crew to the safety of the Rock. But it was not a tidal current; it never reversed. It flowed incessantly, as it had done for thousands of years, from the Atlantic into the Mediterranean, and every vessel that passed from the Mediterranean out to the Atlantic had it to reckon with. Ordinarily, it was no problem. Wait in the harbor of Gibraltar, alongside the squadron of British warships, for a brisk dawn; then sail close to the Spanish shore, where the current was not too swift. But sail that same course on a wild, stormy night? Suicide!

Sheer suicide. Nevertheless, it was what Barney had to do. In the center of the Gut, at night, he would be invisible from either shore; but there the current would be so swift that he would need something better than half a gale to enable the *Sidney* to overcome it by so narrow a margin as a knot or two; so that, if he chose the center, dawn would almost certainly find him sailing furiously against the current and making no headway at all, at a point just off the waiting British warships. And as for the African shore, it swarmed with savage Barbary pirates.

He would need four or five hours of hard sailing from Estepona before he could start his struggle with the current; and since that would require all of the hours of darkness, in midafternoon just after six bells, he weighed anchor and sailed out to meet what had become almost a full easterly gale. Since his course from Estepona to Gibraltar was almost due south, that was as good a wind as he could ask for. Mighty seas pounded the sloping weather side of the *Sidney* as she heeled to the gale, and occasionally one broke clear over her waist and cascaded down her steep deck, to slosh and crash about until it could drain out through the scuppers. The sailors fled into the rigging; the wheel was on the poop deck, out of reach of the seas. The log showed a speed of nine knots. At that rate, Barney estimated, he would come abeam of the Rock before normal dark, and if the weather held, he would almost have to crash into another ship or the Rock before he could see either. He was plunging blindly ahead by dead reckoning, but that was the risk he expected. It was exactly the weather he wanted; he couldn't ask for better.

Three hours later the rain had almost ceased and visibility had increased disturbingly in spite of the later hour. There were no warships in sight and the Rock still was not visible, but it should be about three miles off his starboard quarter. With the wind singing fiercely in his taut rigging and an occasional sea still breaching clear across the waist of the ship, Barney prepared to lay a course between the Rock and the swift center of the current.

In a way, it might have been a comfort to see the Rock; just a fleeting glimpse; just enough to confirm his dead reckoning; but a fresh gust of rain blotted out all but the ship. He assured himself that all was as well as he could wish. He had merely to keep in mind a clear picture of the course between the surf raging around the base of the Rock, and the swift center of the current; and in that picture, to place his ship and to keep her placed. To keep her placed, not only in a picture in his mind, but in fact, on a stormy sea.

The Rock was now, or should be, about three miles off his starboard quarter. He must bring it abeam and keep it so until he began to drop it astern. And to do that, he had to describe a right angle with a radius of about five miles; and he had to do it in total darkness, with a gale driving him swiftly in one direction and a current of increasing force driving him in another.

He could go below and plot the curve on his chart, or he could stay here and do it in his head. Actually, on the chart, it would not be a curve at all. It would be a series of five straight lines, each at an angle of 18 degrees with the preceding line, and each line just 1.5 miles long. On the chart it would be neat and exact, and it would represent the ship as passing just where she should pass. But would those neat pencil lines on the chart control the ship in her battle with wind and sea?

In reality, the problem was not so simple. As he cleared the Rock he would encounter the current. Because the shores of the Gut were not straight and smooth, there would be eddies. The problem would really be a series of equations blending from one into another, to be solved as they developed; and to solve them, he would have to keep his eyes on the compass and his senses attuned to the wind eddying off the Rock and the deck under his feet; and he would have to assemble all of that data as it came to him, and from it to solve those fluid equations by a sort of seaman's instinct. Some veteran seamen do develop such an instinct, but could a boy of sixteen have it? He had to have it. He ordered the first change of course of a point and a half.

He knew very well when he entered the Gut, for the wind eddied off the Rock in wild gusts that veered through 90 degrees, slamming the ship with diabolical cunning and straining every line and spar of her lofty rigging. He must be nearer the Rock than he had supposed for those eddies to be so violent; and he sheered off a mite. Thank God he had a sound ship under him—no such disintegrating wreck as this same current had dragged in out of the Atlantic last February. That current had no affection for a ship it had once rescued; it would save or crush with equal indifference. It was just there, for a man to use if he could.

No British lookout could see him in this howling blackness. No Barbary pirate would venture forth. Most likely he had the Gut entirely to himself. He could give his whole mind to his navigation. He assured himself that all was as well as he could wish.

With the ship running before the wind, no seas boarded

her, and the watch returned to the deck. The slow hours passed, and Barney never left his post. He neither crashed nor was sighted; but not until dawn came to light the sea could he know for certain whether he had passed the squadron of British warships that huddled that night in the lee of the Rock, or whether he would find himself desperately battling the worst of the current in plain sight of the enemy.

Dawn came slowly, imperceptibly at first, over the wild, gray sea, and slowly his field of vision grew. Mr. Barnes stood at the starboard rail, straining his eyes to penetrate the gloom. Joshua wondered if his mate had fully understood the risk he'd run. He appeared to. Good man, Mr. Barnes. When I'm confirmed as master, he thought, I'll keep him on as mate.

The light grew. There was no Rock in sight, no warships off to starboard. Nothing but the storm-tortured sea. The wind had dropped somewhat, and the light still grew. The Rock was out of sight below the curve of the sea or lost in a faint haze astern. More likely the latter, and the *Sidney* was in the area in which the waters of the Atlantic slowly gather themselves together for their headlong rush through the Gut. Her log showed a speed of seven knots, but her actual speed was better than it had been in the Gut—perhaps almost six knots. In another hour she would have left all trace of that current astern.

"Mr. Barnes!" Joshua called.

"Aye, aye, sir!"

"I'm going below to my breakfast, Mr. Barnes. Set all sail to your skysails. Drive her, Mr. Barnes! Drive her! We're homeward bound!"

CHAPTER NINETEEN

ON THE FIRST DAY OF OCTOBER BARNEY CAME ON DECK AT sunrise, as he always did unless bad weather had kept him on deck all night. The *Sidney* was close-hauled on the starboard tack, the wind fresh from the northwest. The ship swooped quartering over the long seas, her lofty mastheads describing intricate curves against the cloud-dappled blue sky, her bows crashing into the waves with swishing thuds so familiar they passed unnoticed, while great fans of spray leaped over the bow and blew spattering down the deck.

The boundless sea and the sky! It satisfied some vague longing deep in the nature of a man. Standing there on his quarter-deck, Barney turned slowly, letting his glance roam at will. The sun's flaming rays splashed gaudy colors over the towering cloud castles of the eastern sky, and flashed on the dancing facets of the sea. The vast blue arch above curved down to meet the white-flecked circle of the restless sea. He thought briefly, contemptuously, of those poor moles he had left behind him in Alexandria, to drudge away their lives in that musty den of a countinghouse. What could a man desire, that he did not already have?

Mr. Barnes greeted his captain with a smile, for Barney kept a happy ship. "Fine mornin', sir. We been loggin' seven knots right along."

"Very good, Mr. Barnes." He concentrated on a simple problem in arithmetic. "If we keep that up, we ought to raise the capes about eight bells. See the lookout keeps an extra sharp eye out forrard."

He hoped to make a good landfall. He expected to. He had been doing it for nearly three years, now. He took pride in telling his officers just what to expect, because it enabled him to demonstrate his mastery of his craft. He enjoyed that. He liked an audience, and his officers and his crew were all he had. Still, for them it was justified, because it increased their confidence in him and was good for discipline.

As eight bells rang, he hailed the masthead. "Lookout, ahoy! Do you see anything?"

"No, sir. I don't see naught!"

The whole crew was eager and excited now, and Barney realized that if he were out in his calculations, this was one time they would never forget, for they had been away for over nine months.

Barney was excited himself, and with good reason, but he was determined not to let his crew see it. He forced himself to wait quietly and impassively, and while he waited, he thought of Mr. Smith, who thought he owned the *Sidney* but didn't, in reality. All Mr. Smith owned were some papers and some ledgers. Barney had the ship. Mr. Smith had never so much as felt her deck heave under his feet. It was Barney who took her out to sea and brought her home. It was his judgment that set her sails or furled them to meet the changing weather. It was his skill as a navigator that charted her position on the trackless waste of water. His feet trod her decks, his mind guided and commanded her, and his heart ached when she labored in dire distress. Mr. Smith, snug at home with his musty ledgers, knew nothing about it. To him she was just an instrument for making money—just a set of entries in his ledgers. To Barney she was a living thing, his pride and joy, the reward for his work and ambition and the symbol of his success. Mr. Smith prized her for her dollar value, but Barney loved her beyond price.

"Land h-o-o-o!" The glad cry floated down from the masthead.

"Where away?"

"One p'int on the sta'b'd bow!" A pause. Then, more excited, "One p'int on the la'b'd bow! One p'int to sta'b'd, one p'int to la'b'd, clear water dead ahead!"

Mr. Barnes looked at his captain in amazement. "Right ker-slap-dab in the center of the capes! How do ye do it, sir?"

Barney shrugged. Latitude just right, longitude just right. No need to tell Mr. Barnes how much of that was luck! Joshua knew he was good, though not that good; but that was something for him to know and Mr. Barnes to find out some day—if the luck didn't hold.

Before noon the *Sidney* passed between the capes into the Chesapeake Bay. The *Gallant Mary* had not been sighted, and that was a strange thing as well as a disappointment, for Barney had been anticipating the pleasure of calling across the water "*Sidney* of Baltimore! Joshua Barney, master!" That would create a sensation on Captain Chilton's little craft.

"Sail broad on the la'b'd bow!" hailed the lookout. A brig she was and just emerging from the sheltering pines at the mouth of the James River. Joshua was not interested in her. Nevertheless, she was approaching rapidly and through his glass Barney saw that she mounted guns. A sloop of war, and flying the British flag! A puff of smoke flared from a bow chaser, and a jet of white water leaped up ahead of the *Sidney*.

"Back your topsails, Mr. Barnes," Barney ordered.

The ship slowed to a stop. A boat loaded with red-coated marines was putting off from the sloop of war, dancing on the seas.

"The bloody pirates!" said Mr. Barnes, his eyes wide with horror. "Is he a-goin' to take us right here in our own Chesapeake, sir?"

"I don't know," Barney replied, determined to remain cool and unruffled on the surface at least, and very thankful that he carried no contraband. "It looks like he might. Put out the ladder."

The effort to appear unmoved set his face in stern lines. He hoped his crew wouldn't guess how helpless he felt. He watched the officer and the marines come over the rail.

The officer posted his men about on the main deck and strode to Barney, who stood on the quarter-deck, awaiting him.

"I want to see the master of this ship!" he said.

"You see him. Captain Barney, sir. What is the meaning of this highhanded boarding in peaceful waters?"

"Not so peaceful, Captain, as you must know. The Colonies are in rebellion. The northern ports are closed and the southern ports are under surveillance. Surely you are aware of the facts."

"I have been away for over nine months, sir. In the Mediterranean most of the time. I'd like to have up-to-date news of this rebellion you speak of."

"You have it, sir. I will look at your papers, Captain."

Seething but helpless, Barney took the officer to his cabin, showed him the log, the manifests and all other papers. The Englishman examined them all with great care. He searched Barney's desk and took possession of the few letters he was carrying for delivery in Baltimore. Then he went on deck and had his marines search the ship. The dozen or so old muskets the *Sidney* carried were brought out, and he took them.

The boarders left at last, and Barney saw the *Gallant Mary* standing by. His pleasure in the meeting was marred by the temper he was in, but he swallowed his anger and hailed Captain Chilton exactly as he had planned to do.

"Joshua, you say you're master now?" the old man called back.

"Aye, sir, since Captain Drysdale died at sea nine months ago."

"Captain Barney, come aboard! Come aboard and tell me all about it!" There was surprise and delight in his old friend's voice. Barney dropped into the boat that had brought him a pilot and was rowed to the *Gallant Mary*, where Captain Chilton's greeting chased away the bad taste left by his encounter with the British.

"Come below, lad, come below. I've sent you my only pilot. You must tell me all about yourself."

For an hour Barney talked while the old man listened. He nodded with understanding over the struggle against sinking; got technical over the repair job; cursed and hooted with delighted laughter over the governor of

Nice; and finally swore that Barney was a credit to him—while the two vessels sailed side by side up the bay. Finally, Captain Chilton visited Barney aboard the *Sidney* and pronounced her as smart a ship from pinrails to skysails as he had ever seen.

The pilot for the run up the bay was Captain Chowning (he called it "Chewning"), a lanky Virginian Barney had known aboard the *Gallant Mary*. He was full of details of Lexington, Concord and Bunker Hill.

"Seems like Massachusetts gets the toughest governors," he said. "That fellow Gage is a general an' he brought an army with him. Seems like he thinks the people of Massachusetts got to obey him like his own soldiers. Course, the harder he cracks down, the harder they fight back."

"I heard the trouble was spreading south while I was still in Spain but I never really believed it. It just didn't seem possible."

"It's spreading, all right," and Captain Chowning gave details of what he called the "ructions" that had already chased southern governors onto British warships.

"Well, now, honestly, Captain Chowning, don't it seem downright ridiculous for us to be squaring off to fight England? What are we going to fight with?"

"There was some people thought if we acted tough enough, England would back down like she done in sixty-five. I reckon they know by now she ain't going to, an' they'd like to know the answer to that question."

"Mr. Smith won't send the *Sidney* to sea again with things like they are," Barney said. He stood silent, gloomily pondering the prospects of this sudden check to his ambitions. He ran his eye forward over his splendid ship; he glanced aloft.

"How about a navy?" he asked at last.

"Navy? Shucks, it ain't even been mentioned, 'sfar's I know. We certainly ain't got one, an' we shore ain't buildin' one."

"When we start building a navy, I'll be ready to believe we're going to war, and not before!" The thought was a comfort.

"Well, we're tryin' to get what we want without fightin', anyway. We've just sort of backed our topsails right now. There's one party in the Congress wants to go slow. They sent a petition to the king to see if he wouldn't listen to reason, an' they're holdin' back, tryin' not to take any more warlike actions, until they hear from that petition. They ain't exactly got everything stopped, but they're mighty slowed down."

"Then maybe we can get what we want without fighting right now?"

"We might."

"When did that petition go out?"

"Last July. The eighth day. But even so, we did make plans for land fightin' right brisk, for a while, there, and we ain't backed down on none of that. The Congress voted to raise a *continental* army. Note that, if you please, sir—a *continental* army. And George Washington of Virginia, sir, was appointed commander in chief of all the troops of all this whole continent. He's up to Boston now an' he's got the lobster-backs bottled up in that city. That's really something, now, I tell you—one army for all these separate colonies. But that was before that petition was sent to the king. Now we just got our topsails backed, waitin'."

"That was nearly three months ago?"

"That's right. And of course, if the king pays attention to that petition Mr. Dickinson wrote for him, everything will be easy again. I don't hold much with politicians, but I must say it was a mighty nice petition, respectful and polite and reasonable, an' a man would have to be lookin' for trouble to ignore it."

An army recruited from all the Colonies, and under a unified command! Rebellion flaring in every colony! Royal governors chased onto British warships! Barney had stopped listening while he tried to digest that astonishing batch of news. Truly the people on the Rock had not known the half of it!

At Whetstone Point Barney saw the first evidence that Baltimore—or Maryland—was preparing for war. A fort had been built on the point, and a boom consisting of three massive chains was stretched across the mouth of the harbor. A narrow channel had been left on the side next to the fort, so that ships must pass directly under its guns to enter the habor. Barney dropped his anchor, ordered out his gig, and had himself rowed rapidly to Mr. Smith's East Pier. He climbed the ladder, strode the length of the pier, crossed Water Street and flung open the door of the countinghouse, where he took Mr. Smith by surprise. In the lordly fashion in which he trod his quarter-deck at sea, he marched in and slammed the door behind him.

At this boisterous intrusion the lean, withered old merchant looked up in irritation. His little gray beard jutting out from his chin, he glared at Barney a moment in silence, completely failing to recognize the proud, self-confident young man as the apprentice boy he had seen without really seeing, possibly, half a dozen times.

"Who in blazes are you, sir?" he demanded indignantly.

"I am Joshua Barney, master of your ship *Sidney*, just arrived."

The old man remembered the name if not the face. "Master of my ship, are you, sir? And how dare you, sir, an apprentice boy, presume to take command of a ship of mine?"

Stung by this harsh greeting, Barney laid his papers on the old man's desk, said, "Read these!" and turning his back, walked to the window.

The old man gave him a sharp glance and settled down, first, to a study of the log. Barney watched people passing in Gay Street. He saw familiar faces, but he did not want to speak to anybody until his status was settled. The old man read on, page after page. Barney tired of watching people. Across Gay Street was a brick building, and to curb his impatience he set himself to count the bricks in the wall. Mr. Smith finished the log and closed it with a bang. He took up receipted bills, invoices, manifests, contracts. Barney tried making epigrams on the names he could see on the signs along Gay Street, then switched his attention to wagons crawling cautiously along the pitted way.

Tired of Gay Street, he walked to the front window and looked out across Water Street to the tidal marsh that stretched a hundred yards to the harbor. Mr. Smith's two long piers, built in the year of Joshua's birth, strode across the wet, rushy mud flat for half their length before their piles stood in water. Skiffs and small sailing craft

246

littered the mud exposed at low tide, and larger vessels lay at anchor in the harbor. It was an old, familiar sight, and held nothing of interest at the moment. Would the old goat never have done with those papers?

Barney walked over to the hearth and stepped on the tail of the huge old dog dozing there, stepped back suddenly at the yelp of anguish, and knocked down the tall iron poker. It fell with a clatter. Mr. Smith paid no attention but read steadily on. Joshua turned his back to the cold fireplace and stood with his hands clasped behind him.

Mr. Smith continued to examine the papers with undiminished concentration until the last one had been read and carefully folded again. Then he rose nimbly from his chair, pushed his glasses up onto his bald head, and loped around the desk, his face all smiles and both hands extended.

"Captain Barney!" he exclaimed, "you are welcome home, sir! I am glad to see you. I congratulate you heartily upon your safe return. Your conduct merits my cordial approbation, sir, and I am proud to find that I have so deserving a young man in my employ. Take a seat, sir. Take a seat. We'll see what's to be done immediately."

It was a strangely somber Captain Joshua Barney who stepped onto the plank sidewalk in front of Mr. Smith's countinghouse two hours later. Of all that Mr. Smith had told him about the turbulence raging in the thirteen colonies, two facts stood out.

The first was that the *Sidney* would do no more voyaging until peace could be restored.

The second was that the Colonies not only had no navy but did not seem to think that one would be necessary.

A sea captain without a ship, ashore in a colony that

247

was going to war without a navy—could a man find himself in a more futile position?

Given a navy, an ambitious man could win glory in a war for independence, but without a navy . . . !

At the livery stable around the corner from Gay Street he hired a saddle horse and set out for home.

To build a navy—he shook his head in despair. A war could be finished before a navy could be built. Gloomily he let his nag take her own pace out the North Point Road. The triumphant return home that he had anticipated with such relish was proving to be a dull business. It was not in Barney's nature, though, to remain gloomy for long. After all, war might be averted—and wasn't he already the master of a great ship? And hadn't he magnificent tales to tell at home? His spirits rebounded. He whipped up his horse, and he finished the eight-mile ride with a very satisfactory clatter of hoofs on the white oystershell lane of the plantation.